Joel took a deep breath. "Would you go to the Homecoming Dance with me?" he asked.

If my face didn't register my shock, my hands surely did. I lost control of my books, and they crashed to the floor all around our feet.

I quickly turned all my attention to those books so Joel couldn't see the confusion and embarrassment on my face. I tried to stall for time. *What would Elaine say if I went to the dance with Joel? Ha! What wouldn't she say?*

Then I surprised myself by saying, "Yes, I'd like to go with you, Joel. Thank you."

Walking home, I couldn't keep my mind from spinning. I kept thinking, *Wow! I've got a date for homecoming!*

But how will I ever tell my best friend that it's with the guy she hates most in the whole school?

Key to ♥ My Heart

VICTORIA M. ALTHOFF

Photo by John Strange

Published by Willowisp Press, Inc.
401 E. Wilson Bridge Road, Worthington, Ohio 43085

Printed in the United States of America
10 9 8 7 6 5 4 3 2

ISBN 0-87406-384-1

To David,
who understands
the dream and the
dangerous job. Thank you
for sharing encouragement,
love, courage, horrible puns,
and pots of tea.

One

"STAND up, Pockel," Bud Brandis instructed as he gave Horatio, my saxophone, a slap.

I jerked my head up to stare at the tanned face, wire-rimmed glasses, and sun-streaked, brown hair that hung over the sweaty forehead of my section leader. He grinned at me with that wicked smile of his. It was one of Bud's typical put-downs.

I yanked Horatio away from him and suppressed an urge to yell, "I am standing up!" I knew I couldn't answer him, though, because whenever Bud says anything to me, my vocal cords turn into pillow feathers. Bud chuckled and went to his place in the lineup while I fumed at myself.

Ginger Pockel, where are all those great words when you want them? I asked myself. Well, at least Bud had noticed me. Now if

7

he'd just use my first name instead of my last, so I wouldn't feel like a can of generic vegetables. I wouldn't even mind a nickname like "Gingersnap" if Bud used it. Well, maybe I would mind just a little.

We walked onto the football field and started marking time in the hot sunshine. I counted *one, two, step, two* as we progressed down the field. "For just a cold shower and a frosted mug of lemonade," I muttered under my breath, "today I'd give up marching band, my saxophone, and even this chance to be near Bud Brandis."

But even as I mumbled those thoughts, I knew they weren't true. We all were practicing hard because our director, Mr. Cavatina, was afraid we wouldn't be ready for the first football game that was in two weeks. Everyone loved performing for the games, but right now my hair hung hot and heavy against my neck, and my glasses kept slipping down my nose. Heat waves shimmered in ghostlike clouds above the field. One *of these days,* I thought, *the whole band will melt into a mirage, never to be seen again.*

Mr. Cavatina mopped his red face with his already-sweaty handkerchief and shouted, "Okay, let's do the pre-game segment straight through one time!"

8

Even though I have to look up at him, Mr. Cavatina is not a big man. But he does have a loud voice that bellows out from beneath that dark mustache. If he wasn't the best high school band director in Ohio, I could easily picture him as an actor. Today I'd cast him as a villain for making us practice in this heat. I pulled my hair up off of my neck for a few seconds. *Why hadn't I worn a hair clip? I hope Bud can't tell how sweaty I am,* I thought.

Squad leaders called, "Heads up! Left foot first! Let's get it right this time!"

I swung Horatio back and forth in rhythm. Maybe it's a little odd to see me carrying a tenor saxophone that dangles to my knees, but I love the wonderful, deep sound that Horatio makes. It was an added bonus when I got into the band to discover that Bud Brandis, a guy I'd liked since we were both in middle school, was my section leader.

He was two places behind me now, looking tall and lean. His glasses and straight, brown hair made him look intellectual. By turning my head slightly, I could watch him as he marched down the field. Suddenly, he leaned forward. My heart danced against my rib cage. *Maybe he was going to talk to me!*

But he didn't. Instead, he tapped the shoulder of Cynthia Semple who was in the

9

other line, and whispered something into her ear. When she turned to him, he tweaked her nose familiarly. My heart sank. *Isn't it odd how you can suddenly feel cold on a hot day?* A shiver ran all the way down my back to my toes as I watched them.

Cynthia always dressed with style. She was wearing an adorable denim outfit, which was coordinated with the latest in silver accessories. Even though she sits at the bottom of the flute section and gets only average grades, Cynthia does know how to dress. She also has strawberry blond curls, the color my parents thought my hair was going to be when they named me Ginger. *How come Cynthia never looks hot and sweaty?* I fumed to myself.

The drummers did some exaggerated stick twirling and started the steady beat that we all march to. It echoed through my whole body, and we began to march across the field. In the excitement, I forgot about the heat. It definitely was great being a part of the famous Middlebrook Marching 100.

Step, turn, step, turn, I repeated to myself as we marched. We filed out of that formation and began forming another as we swung our instruments in sync to catch the light and turned with military precision. Freshly applied yard line chalk swirled in the air.

Across the steamy field, I could see Elaine Fabiani, who looked equally as hot as I was. Elaine is my best friend, and the only freshman in the first clarinet section. She has the highest grades in the class, and I think she is gorgeous. Her olive complexion has never showed a zit. And she has black hair, dark eyes, and curves in all the right places. I guess Elaine could have Bud falling all over her if she wanted.

By contrast, I'm kind of short. I guess the first thing anyone notices about me is the part on top of my head. I have brown hair that seems to curl in all the wrong places, and pretty, green eyes that are camouflaged by glasses. I try not to think about why Bud isn't crazy about me, but I admit that it's not an easy thing to forget about.

We marched down the field and automatically began forming an *M* figurine. I saw that Bob Stewart was on the wrong yard line. I gestured to him. He swung his tuba around, marched over to me, did a three-quarter turn, and that's the last thing I remember. There was a sudden pain above my right ear, and I felt the thud of metal against my skull. Horatio slipped from my hands, and I staggered as the sky went green and the grass went yellow. When I realized I was out of step,

I grabbed the sax that was dangling from my neck strap and hurried into position just as the song ended.

"Ginger Pockel!" Mr. Cavatina bellowed. "What is that you're doing? Is it some new dance step? We're supposed to be marching. Perhaps you'd care to teach your method to us."

I felt my face grow hot. I stared at the ground and shook my head. Behind me, people were beginning to laugh. Bob raised his hand, but Mr. Cavatina had changed subjects by then.

"Trombones, you're the front line. Get those slides up. You're not supposed to dig a trench in the field." He paused. "All right, people. I know it's hot. Let's play the National Anthem and then call it a day."

After the last run-through, I gathered my things together and trudged toward the band room. Bud stormed up behind me. "Can't you do anything right, Pockel?" he yelled. Two narrow locks of brown hair fell over his forehead. His cheeks were red enough to hide the fine line of freckles beneath his glasses.

I just stood there. I couldn't say anything. Hurt and anger swelled inside me like a pill I couldn't swallow, and tears welled up in my eyes. *Why did I always make him mad?*

Couldn't he see that he was hurting me? Didn't he care, even a little?

"Leave her alone, Brandis. It was my fault," Bob Stewart said in my defense. But Bud had stalked off already. "Are you all right, Ginger?" Bob asked.

"Huh?" I mumbled as I watched Bud slip into step beside Cynthia. It took a minute to realize that Bob was talking. "Oh, sure," I said. "It's nothing, Bob."

"I guess I hit you pretty hard with my tuba when I swung around. I must have looked right over your head and not even seen you. I didn't realize that you're so short."

Bob is like a block of granite. If I look straight at him, I barely see over his belt buckle. Despite his remark, Bob is one of the nicest people in the band. I just wished that he would forget the subject of my height.

"It's okay," I repeated as we entered the school. The cool, dark halls were a relief after a full day of bright sunshine and that strawlike football field. When we got to the band room, I carefully packed Horatio into his case and collected my backpack. Elaine was talking, or rather listening, to Mr. Cavatina and a boy I'd never seen before. The looks on their faces signaled that it was a private conversation.

The boy beside Elaine was about the same

height as she was. He was short, and he was built well. His hair was even blacker than hers, but he had blue eyes. Even from this distance, his eyes looked almost too blue. He noticed that I was staring at him, and the corner of his lip twitched into a small smile. I felt my cheeks get hot, and I quickly decided to wait for Elaine outside in the hall.

There was a rush and clatter as the rest of the band members cleared out of the band room. Then the hallway became empty and quiet. Yet, Elaine did not appear. Finally, I peeked into the band room in time to see the boy shake Elaine's hand.

He bent forward stiffly almost into a bow. There was something strange about the whole scene. It made me think of fencers getting ready to duel. But then, I'm a big fan of 19th-century adventure novels.

Elaine sensed that I was there and turned toward the door. The boy turned to speak privately to Mr. Cavatina. He seemed unusually interested in this new guy.

I'm probably the only one in the world who knows Elaine well enough to realize that she was mad. Her smile looked like a Halloween mask, and her step was stiff, as if she was still marching.

"What's up?" I asked.

"Wait until we get out of here," she replied through clenched teeth.

As we started down the hallway, I felt a prickle in the back of my neck and turned to look behind us. The boy stood by the band room door, staring at us. The right side of his mouth curled into a half smile. He tilted his head and nodded to me. Those blue eyes were incredible! They seemed to be assessing me like a shopper examines fruit in the produce market. Suddenly, his smile seemed so persistent that I turned away fast.

Two

"THE nerve! The very nerve of him!" Elaine exploded when we were outside of the band room.

"Either that blue-eyed boy or Mr. Cavatina is on your nerves," I observed.

For once, she didn't even grimace at me. Her sandals made a short, sharp smack against the pavement. I had to run to keep up. My sax case banged against my leg.

"Do you know what he did?" Elaine stormed at me.

"Who?" I asked.

"Mr. Cavatina!"

"Well, no, I don't," I admitted.

"This kid—this *new kid*—comes in, and Mr. Cavatina puts him in the first clarinet section right below me. He's in *my* squad without even having to try out. And what's worse is that I'm supposed to help him get adjusted."

"Who? Mr. Cavatina?" I asked.

"And I have to show him the ropes. Can you believe it?"

"Who?" I asked, beginning to feel a lot like an owl.

"That guy! Honestly, Ginger, pay attention," she said. "His name is Joel." She gave me a look of complete exasperation. "And Mr. Cavatina didn't even say a word about the whole week of practice that Joel had missed."

That was definitely odd. People who missed practice became alternates. And nobody got to the first-chair position of the clarinets that easily. Even Elaine, who is a terrific musician, had to work really hard to earn first-chair clarinetist. She only has the first-chair position because Tom Oaks and Rich Schaffer are on the football team. There are 23 clarinetists, which I think is an excellent reason for playing the saxophone.

To change positions within a section, a person has to challenge someone who's at a higher level in the section. Mr. Cavatina listens to each of them play, and then he chooses the better player for the top position, or first-chair position.

I would never be able to challenge anyone. Bud and Brian Wells, who are both juniors, play first and second tenor saxophone. And besides, playing for Mr. Cavatina turns my lip into mush and my hands into klutzy blobs.

"It doesn't make any sense," I replied.

"He didn't even have to try out, the little twerp!" Elaine repeated her earlier comment. "Mr. Cavatina has no right to make me baby-sit him."

"Who is he, anyway?" I asked as we came to my house. I held the door open for Elaine and then followed her inside.

"I don't know," she said. "Joel Woodstock, or Stockwood, or Woodstack, or something. He's just transferred here. I don't know why he's allowed to start practice so late in the season."

Elaine made me wonder if the new kid got teased about his name, too. "Okay," I said, "think of why Mr. Cavatina would make him first-chair clarinet." I peered into the refrigerator. "Do you want a salami sandwich?"

"Yeah, I'm starved," she said. "But that's what really gets me. I don't understand why Mr. Cavatina would do it, either." We ate sandwiches and tried to guess why Mr. Cavatina would promote the new kid to first-chair clarinet. Well, *I* tried to figure it out. Elaine wasn't being rational. I should have suspected right then that Elaine was upset about something, but I didn't.

"Maybe Stackedwood, or whoever he is, is blackmailing Mr. Cavatina," I said in my best cloak-and-dagger voice.

Elaine gave me her "enough is enough" look. "What for?" she asked.

I tried to sound dramatic, which is not easy with a mouthful of salami and mustard. "His father is a music publisher. He's found out how we photocopy all the extra music parts. You know how each one says not to reproduce under penalty of death by stabbing with a baton. So he's threatened to sue Mr. Cavatina unless his darling Joel can play first-chair clarinet."

Elaine rolled her eyes and then grumbled, "Really, Ginger, this is serious." The way Elaine rolls her eyes and tosses her head back really bugs me. She believes that a freshman should be sophisticated. Elaine has had more dates than I have. But that's not too difficult, because I haven't had any.

Since I want to attract Bud, I try to do everything Elaine says is necessary for getting a date. I wear makeup, and I try to remember to walk, not dash, to classes. But I keep forgetting to change from my scruffy tennis shoes to short heels after band. Elaine's head and eye gestures are her way of saying I'm not what I ought to be. *Boy, that really makes me mad.*

"Well, there's nothing I can do about Wood-stack," I said.

Just then, the back door opened, and Dad appeared in the doorway. "How was practice?" he asked cheerfully.

"Hot!" I told him. "We're having salami sandwiches. Do you want one?"

Dad wrinkled his nose. "Sure, are you fixing them?"

Dad sat down at the table and asked Elaine about her day. She perked up a little, and some of her gray mood left her eyes. Dad is great at cheering up people. He's the advertising sales manager of the *Brookview Morning Chronicle*, so I suppose he's naturally friendly. Sometimes he stops home to have lunch with Mom. She usually gets home early from her part-time bookkeeping job at a nearby attorneys' office.

I handed Dad his sandwich. "Ginger, have you heard from Mom?" he asked.

"No," I said, "but in the refrigerator there's a casserole with a note attached that says, '350 degrees at 3:30.' "

"She must be pretty busy today if she's trying to be that organized," Dad said with a whistle. "Well, are you two ready for school to start?"

"The band isn't ready," Elaine said. "We all were stumbling around out there today."

"And how are the boys this year?" Dad teased her. Elaine grinned. *Maybe Elaine should be Dad's daughter,* I thought. *Then he could be proud of her grades.* But even Elaine might get tired of all those hints about a career in newspaper writing.

"They're tan, tall, and good-looking," Elaine laughed. "Now, if we can just get them to notice us."

Dad smiled. "Well, the motto in my business is 'It pays to advertise,' but in looking for boyfriends you really can't rely only on advertisements.

We giggled as he finished his sandwich. "Well, I have to get back to work." At the door, he turned back to Elaine. "Ginger's taking journalism this year, Elaine. Are you?"

She shook her head. "I couldn't work it into my schedule. Have a good day, Mr. Pockel."

I knew Elaine didn't want to take journalism. But she didn't say that to Dad, who thinks journalism is the only course in high school that is worth taking.

We went up to my room. Last year, Dad remodeled the attic into a large room for me. One end of the room has bookshelves that cover the wall from the floor to the ceiling.

"I love your room, Ginger," Elaine said. Her dark eyes flickered over the travel posters taped to the slanted ceiling, and she glanced at the books that were crammed onto the bookshelves. "I wish my parents would let me move into our attic. Your bookshelves are great, and I love the way your desk folds into the wall."

"When it comes to books and writing materials, I have everything I need," I said. "It's okay, but all I've heard is journalism ever since I was old enough to hold a pencil."

"Ginger, your parents are so special. Your dad even teases us about boys. I wish I could talk with my parents that way. Whenever I go out with someone, my dad questions him to death, and my mom tries to fatten him up with pasta."

"Your parents *are* strict," I admitted, "but they let you make up your own mind about what courses you take at school."

She shrugged and curled her hair around her finger. "Anyway, your dad is right about our needing to advertise. How are we going to get the boys to notice us, Ginger?"

I conjured up a mental picture of Bud staring at me admiringly. I tried to picture him smiling appreciatively. But I could only come up with an angry scowl like he had this afternoon when Bob Stewart knocked me out of position.

"Well, I'm going to be the new me," I said as I sat up straight. "I'm going to brush my hair every period to make it stay right, and I'm getting rid of these stupid glasses."

"That's the way to go!" Elaine enthused. "But how are you going to get rid of your glasses?"

"I'm getting contact lenses. I've been saving my baby-sitting money for almost a year."

"Wow, Ginger! That's super. When are you going to buy them?"

"I've already ordered them."

"Why didn't you tell me?" she pouted.

I shrugged. "I was saving the surprise," I said.

"Take off your glasses, and let me see," Elaine ordered.

I did, and the room became a blur. I could tell she was wrinkling her nose by the funny sound of her voice.

"Well, you'll just have to use more makeup now," she said slowly.

I giggled and put on my glasses.

"Well, Ginger, everyone will notice *you,* but what will *I* do to get Ryan's attention?"

"Ryan who?" I asked. "I thought you were interested in Todd Saunders. Or did our trombone player slide out of your grasp?"

She made a face and laughed. "Todd was last year, when I wanted to be with somebody in high school. Now that I'm in high school, too, I'd like to date a senior. They're so interesting. Besides, I think Ryan Wright's curly, brown hair is so cute.

"So, Ryan Wright is Mr. Right for now, huh?" I asked. "What makes you think seniors will care about us? We're only freshmen. Even the sophomores think we're awful."

"The sophomores are the awful ones," Elaine said wisely. "Seniors are mature. They can recognize our good qualities."

I didn't say anything.

"And who are you going to flirt with now that you'll have new contact lenses?" Elaine smirked, "as if I didn't know."

I blushed. "Well..."

"Get smart, Ginger," Elaine frowned. "Bud Brandis is a junior. He isn't particularly good-looking, and he's sarcastic and moody. He also likes Cynthia Semple. That ought to tell you something about him right there."

"Well, I think Bud is handsome. He's also clever and witty. And he's president of the Debate Team."

Elaine rolled her eyes. "Ginger, Bud doesn't like smart girls, or he wouldn't hang around with Cynthia. Get it?"

"Maybe he doesn't know how nice it would be to have someone to talk with," I suggested hopefully.

Elaine threw up her hands. "Well, I can't choose your boyfriends for you." She shook her head and sighed. "All right, how do you plan to focus his attention on your good qualities?"

"I don't know," I admitted. I was trying to think of what my good qualities were.

Elaine said, "Well, let's find a way to advertise."

"Do you mean we should wear T-shirts that say 'I'm available'?" I asked.

"No, I mean, we should do something really crazy. We shouldn't do anything stupid, but something to set us apart from the other girls."

"Maybe we could name our instruments or something? Well, no," I said, remembering that we did that last year. "By the way, you are going to share a locker with me this year, aren't you?"

"Sure," Elaine said. Then she got a strange, really devilish, look in her eyes. "That's it!" she cried. Suddenly she jumped up and reached for some paper in my desk. "We'll decorate our locker in some crazy way."

I shook my head. "Do you mean like using balloons and streamers? You've got to be kidding, Elaine."

"No, Ginger, I'm not." She carried the paper and markers to the large, round table in the corner of my room and sat down. "We'll make signs, like the protest signs that people used to hold up at political rallies in the '60s and '70s. But our causes will be different than theirs were."

I knew that we would look different all right. Everyone has to share a dark green locker. If the inside of our locker was filled with bright signs, it would really show up. "But we don't want it to look dumb," I objected.

"No, it will just look clever," Elaine replied. Already she was writing on a piece of yellow construction paper. "We'll invent slogans, like 'Down with—' "

"—gravity," I finished the slogan without thinking.

"And up with elevators," she added, beaming.

"Trust me," she grinned, and her dark eyes flashed with mischief.

Three

BUD Brandis was leaning over my shoulder to read our signs. I gazed up at him. I felt his breath near my face. *He was that close to me.* My mind was turning like a corkscrew. This was the first time he'd actually spoken to me since school started three days ago. I'd been planning this encounter since we had put up the signs in our locker.

"George Washington slept here?"

I took a deep breath, and quipped, "Yeah, that was probably the last time the place was cleaned out."

Bud's shirt reflected a blue edge onto those brown eyes. "That's clever, Pockel," he said slowly. "What happened to your glasses?"

"I have contact lenses now," I managed to stutter, trying not to grin with the joy I felt from being noticed. Never mind that my eyes were red and watery, I knew I looked much better without glasses. And now Bud was noticing, too. Suddenly, I realized I had nothing else to say to Bud. And still he stood there, staring. Maybe he was appreciating my new makeup and soft pink blouse. Or, maybe he was just reading the signs on the locker door. I groped frantically for something else to say.

"We still have billboard space for rent," I started to say as Cynthia Semple strutted down the hall toward us.

"Oh, Bud, I'm so glad I caught you," she gushed. *Caught was right,* I thought, *because she reminded me of a black widow spider.* In her black sweater and skirt, dangling silver earrings, and dark stockings, Cynthia looked like a spider. And in 10 seconds, she had easily wrapped her web around Bud. "Bud, it's this English class, and all those propositions." She shook her head to make the earrings swing.

Bud pivoted away from me, mesmerized. Smiling, he walked right into her net. I was too upset to hear what they were saying. I didn't mind that Cynthia ignored me, but having Bud ignore me was different.

"That's prepositions!" I shouted behind them, correcting Cynthia. I grabbed my physical science book and slammed the locker shut.

The clang echoed down the hallway.

"It serves it right, huh Ginger?" Joel Stockwood materialized behind me, and I jumped. I had carefully avoided him, since the day Mr. Cavatina introduced him, and Elaine had received her bad news about Joel sharing the position of first-chair clarinet with her. I didn't even know he knew my name.

"Excuse me?" I mumbled. My mind was not on Joel Stockwood today. I was busy envying Cynthia. *How did she do it? How did Cynthia so deliberately play helpless? And why did Bud heel like a puppy?*

"My locker is tough to shut, too." Joel interrupted my thoughts. I glanced down the hall and hoped Elaine wouldn't see me with him. She really was mad at this guy for jumping positions in the section. I had heard that other kids weren't too happy about it either.

But Joel couldn't read my thoughts, so he just kept on talking. "I guess it's this old building. If I don't slam my locker, it won't latch either."

What was he talking about? I wondered. *I was worrying about Bud, and he thought I was having trouble with my locker! And what was that remark about an old building? He was the newcomer. If he didn't like it, he could leave.* I thought of just walking away, but I'm not the type to do that. Instead, I looked into his blue eyes that were so clear, honest, and deep. I shivered.

He smiled, and his eyes crinkled into half moons. But he had a knowing look, as if he thought I'd fall madly in love with him at any minute. "Where are you going?" he asked.

"I have physical science right now," I muttered, and then gulped, because he gave me a funny look when I said "physical." He looked too confident, as if he was older than the rest of us already. I told myself I wasn't about to be overwhelmed by any charms Joel might think he had. Besides, my best friend really didn't like him.

"I'm headed for geography," he commented as we started down the hall. "You know, it's nice walking with someone who looks up to me."

Not him, too, I thought as we kept walking. Then I realized that Joel probably didn't know anybody except for a few people in band, and one of them was Elaine. Her conversation with him was bound to be as friendly as my talks with Bud were.

He swung his books to the other hand, which put us closer together. I knew Elaine disliked him, but Joel must feel lonely. So I smiled. "How do you like your classes?" I asked.

"They're okay, I guess. There aren't many kids from band in them, though."

I thought so, I told myself. *He's lonesome.* "Did you just move to town?" I asked.

"No, I went to Northbrook Middle School last year, but my music teacher suggested that I apply to Middlebrook High."

"Why? Because it helps to play in a better band?" I asked. I had heard that before. Kids apply especially to Middlebrook because of our music program. Each year, some Middlebrook band kids get professional jobs in orchestras, or win music scholarships to college.

"No," he said. He didn't add "stupid," but the deep sarcasm in his voice did. "I needed Cavatina's harmony class, and Northbrook High doesn't have one. Actually, my teacher didn't want me to join the band, especially not the marching band." He stared at me as if I didn't know anything. "You know, stomping around the football field just to fill the time between halves of a football game really is a waste of time. It ruins your lip for serious playing."

"Oh, well," I interrupted. "I suppose for someone as great as you, it's a real problem to put up with the rest of us, isn't it?" Then, before he could say anything else, I turned the corner and went into my physical science class.

So that's what Elaine meant. *What makes him think he's too good for Middlebrook, or for the rest of us? And, for that matter, how did he get to first-chair clarinet without even trying out?* Joel Stockwood, I had decided, was conceited and a pain. And I didn't care if he ever found a friend.

Four

THE idea of band competitions isn't high on Mr. Cavatina's priority list. He thinks it's more important for band members to enjoy football season and the thrill of entertaining during half time. But our dedication to our shows has earned us respect, and Joel Stockwood's attitude made me mad. I couldn't wait to tell Elaine that she was right about him, but I didn't get the chance to do that in physical science because we had a surprise quiz. I couldn't believe it. *We had a test on the third day of school!*

When my day starts out crummy, it usually stays that way. When I finally got the chance to talk with Elaine at lunch, she just nodded smugly. "What did I tell you, Ginger? He thinks he's God's gift to the clarinet. And I even have to sit next to him every day. It's terrible." She moved on to other subjects, and soon the lunch bell rang.

The best part of my day is journalism class. This year I have it during eighth period. I really just took the course to please Dad, but Ms. Dyre, our teacher, is young, pretty, and a lot of fun.

Today, she showed us the big glass "dummy" boards for pasting up the newspaper pages. "Next week, we'll go on a field trip to a print shop," she told us, amidst cheers from the class.

She talked about how to write a news story. Through the classroom window, I could see the practice field. My imagination began to wander, and images of Joel began to appear as I remembered how perfect he thought he was. *I suppose Joel is so perfect that he doesn't have to practice.*

"Ginger Pockel, can you tell us?" Ms. Dyre asked me. I brought my mind back to the present and saw that she was staring at me, waiting for the answer. I had no idea what answer she wanted. I shook my head and felt my cheeks grow hot with embarrassment.

Ms. Dyer said, "Well, who was listening and can help Ginger with the answer?"

Fred Bellows answered, "The answer is who, what, when, where, and why, Ms. Dyre."

"Don't forget to include how, Fred. But, yes,

that's what your story must tell," she said.

I played with my pencil, squirming with embarrassment. *Ginger,* I grumbled to myself, *if you don't pay attention, you'll soon be like Cynthia.* That was not the way I planned to attract Bud.

"You will receive an assignment each week, and also some long-term projects that will require you to do a little more digging for information," Ms. Dyre went on. "So, besides the short article you will do this week, you can begin thinking about a feature story on your favorite class. You could interview the teacher, other students, or just write about how you feel about the class. Let's make it due on October first, the Monday after homecoming."

"What if we don't have a favorite subject?" Fred asked.

"Then interview a janitor," replied Ms. Dyre.

The class snickered, but Ms. Dyre looked up sharply. "I wasn't joking. Every person has a story to tell. You can make any topic or subject interesting. It is your writing that will determine whether a newspaper is read."

Ms. Dyre is a good teacher. Even when she's angry or disappointed with us, she only wants to make us work harder. But I felt confused like Fred did about picking a favorite subject. What in the world did I have to write about for class?

"I'm expecting great things from you," Ms. Dyre said to the class. "There are some contests I've been reading about, and if any of your stories are standouts, perhaps we can compete in them."

Joel Stockwood was waiting for me by the lockers after class. *What a great end to a perfect day*, I muttered sarcastically as I walked toward him.

"Ginger, when we were talking this morning, I didn't mean to sound like I hated band," he hurried to tell me.

I doubted my opinion could make any difference to Mr. Perfect. But I said, "Don't worry about it."

Joel, however, wouldn't let it go at that. "I mean it," he said. "*I* didn't say those things. My teacher did. I wouldn't want to miss band."

"Really?" I asked sarcastically. I was tired of being nice to people. "Look, Joel," I said, "it makes no difference to me. When you're on that field, you'd better do the best you can, even if you think you're better than us."

His lips tightened into an angry line. "I said I didn't mean it. I thought I owed you an apology, but I see I was wrong."

He walked away, and I instantly felt bad for being so mean. "Joel!" I started after him. When he stopped, I called, "I'm sorry! I just had a rotten day."

He shrugged. "Forget it," he said, but he still looked mad.

*   *   *   *   *

"Stand up, Pockel," Bud Brandis said as we lined up in the chilly sunlight the next morning. This afternoon was going to be hot and humid, but at this early hour we shivered. "Do you know what?" Bud turned to Brian Wells. "Pockel is so short that I bet if she sat on the ground, her feet would dangle."

They didn't talk to me directly. They just talked about me as if I wasn't there. "You can tell Pockel likes red," Bud told Brian. "Her name, her temper, and now even her eyes are red."

Suddenly, I didn't feel pretty anymore, not even with the contact lenses. "Shut up," I said, and tried to keep my bottom lip from quivering.

"Watch out, Bud," Brian grinned. "She snaps. Do you get it? Gingersnaps!"

I couldn't stand to hear Bud make cruel

remarks about me. I knew I would make a fool of myself if I sat there one more minute. I grabbed my sax and went to the instrument room in a hurry. Luckily, the period was nearly over. Mr. Cavatina didn't say anything. I hoped I could get out of there before Bud arrived.

"Ginger!" Joel stopped me just outside the doorway. I wanted to keep walking. But Bud was coming toward us. If he said one more thing, I was sure to start crying. I turned to Joel so that Bud wouldn't bother me.

"What is it?" I hoped my eyes could hold the water that was welling up in them.

"Look, I haven't said anything right since I met you. Could we start over? I'd like to be friends."

In my angry mood, I could barely stand to look at those clear blue eyes. "Uh, sure," I managed to say, noticing that Bud was only three feet away, putting away his sax.

"Good," Joel said and grinned.

When I looked at that smile, suddenly the icicles fell off my brain. Joel seemed nice enough. When the bell rang, Joel grabbed his books, and we started down the hallway.

"Listen, Ginger," Joel was saying, "can I ask you a favor?"

"What?"

"I'll understand if you say no. Uh, could I borrow your saxophone to try out for the jazz band?" he asked. "If I make it, my folks will let me rent one, but I need a sax to try out."

It was the last thing in the world I expected. I just stared at him. He must have misunderstood me, because he went right on, "Hey, forget it. People shouldn't borrow instruments. I shouldn't have asked."

"No, it's okay, Joel," I said. "I don't mind."

"You mean it? Gosh, thanks. I'll take care of it. I promise."

Elaine was not going to like this, I thought. I wasn't too fond of Joel, but I did feel guilty about being so mean yesterday. Besides, he might beat out Bud and Brian for one of their seats, and at this moment I'd like nothing better. I saw Elaine ahead of us. "Uh, excuse me, Joel," I said, "I want to talk with Elaine." Joel was still thanking me as I hurried away.

"Were you talking to the enemy?" Elaine greeted me sourly.

"He wanted to apologize," I explained, "and he wants to borrow Horatio for the jazz band tryouts."

"That explains it," Elaine said with a wise nod.

"It explains what?"

"It explains why he would apologize. He

wouldn't eat his words without wanting something in return."

She didn't say anything I hadn't thought of myself. Someone with Joel's ego wouldn't go out of his way to make friends with me unless he wanted something. Well, I decided, that was Joel's problem, not mine. But my stomach suddenly felt like I had eaten paperweights for breakfast.

In the middle of physical science class, I noticed that I still wore my ratty tennis shoes and my saxophone neck strap from band practice. I noticed the band strap because its hook caught on the faucet handle and created a fountain during Mr. Sorenson's lecture. He just stared at me until I got myself untangled, which made everyone else stare, too.

I quickly stuffed my neck strap into my pocket. Then I realized that if I pretended to forget I had the strap, Joel wouldn't be able to try out today. It is impossible to play a tenor sax without the strap. Elaine would be happy that Joel didn't get into the jazz band, and I could just say it was a mistake.

But I couldn't do it. I even risked being late to math by running to the band room at the beginning of fifth period. I pushed open the door and was startled to see that everything had been changed around. The familiar semicircle of chairs was shoved aside to make room for a different arrangement of the music stands. Tall guys hurried in and out of the instrument room, dragging the bass viola and the trap drum set. I felt strange being in the band room when it wasn't for band. I turned to leave just as Joel came through the door.

He frowned. "You changed your mind," he guessed.

"No," I said softly, feeling the blush begin. I shoved the neck strap at him. "Here," I said. "Good luck, and my sax is named Horatio."

I hurried out. The last I saw, Joel was shaking his head and looking at the neck strap in his hand.

Five

PERFORMING for the first game of the season always makes everyone in the band nervous. By 6:30, we were pacing around the band room, straightening our uniforms and positioning our hats. All of us were early. The air was filled with nervous excitement and the smell of dry-cleaning fluid from the uniforms.

Todd Saunders was going over the fight song with Clarence White, a freshman trombonist in his line. Bud wouldn't have thought to give me extra help. I looked for Elaine, but the drums called us to practice.

Bud was in the flute row, absorbed in adjusting Cynthia's necktie. I wondered how Cynthia could look good even in a baggy band uniform.

Mr. Cavatina tapped his baton for attention. We got quiet. Bud walked over to our section, still ignoring me. Mr. Cavatina said, "You've worked hard these past weeks. You're not just individuals now. Together you've become an impressive band. You know your stuff. Just relax, and do the job I know you can do."

We lined up for pre-game in two long rows in the twilight behind the stadium. Pre-game is really just the way we get onto the field to play the National Anthem. But at Middle-brook, the band makes an elaborate show of it. People walked around us carrying hot dogs and drinks.

Bill Hardin, our drum major, called us to attention, and it suddenly was quiet all around us. I could hear Brian Wells, behind me, breathing hard. My forehead was sweating under the heavy hat. I jammed it down so it wouldn't fall off. The drummers marched onto the field. Then we moved out for my first pre-game.

The two lines split apart, and each person marched two steps ahead of the next one, along the sides of the field. Then each person turned and filed into his row until the whole band formed a block. There was the soft crunch of marching feet.

I continued counting and marching, and then I realized that something was wrong. The trombones were five yards in front of every-one else. They had gone too many rows! There were hurried shouts, and then we stepped off for the fight song. The trombones just kept their five-yard distance in front of the clarinets. *Todd was smart,* I thought. If he had tried to get his line to wait for the band to catch up, some of the rows might not have started right.

The trombones moved to their proper yard line when we changed to the *block M* forma-tion. Then the crowd of voices blended with our music for *The Star Spangled Banner.* The sound reached high into the night, raising goose bumps on my arms beneath my uniform.

Middlebrook's band has its own bleachers at one end of the field. We can barely see anything from there. I usually don't care for football, but the school games are different.

The other girls, like Elaine, try to be mature and act like scoring a touchdown or winning are no big deal. *This year,* I told myself, *I'd be that way, too.* I repeated that to myself as I watched Cynthia pat a space next to her and Bud sit down.

But about two minutes into the game, Paul Sproul, who sits behind me in English class, caught a long pass and ran for a touchdown at the far end of the field. Nobody tried to block him. Nobody even came near him!

"Ginger, will you sit down before you fall off the bleachers with all that jumping?" Elaine cried irritably.

"I was not jumping," I said calmly, and looked around to see if anyone had noticed. Nobody at all had noticed me.

I decided I had been stupid to worry about Joel being lonely. He had a whole circle of clarinet players sitting around him, and they were all talking and laughing. Elaine muttered, "Look at him over there. He may be good at the clarinet, but he sure doesn't hesitate to tell everybody about it."

I wondered how she knew what he was saying several seats away. "Maybe it pays to advertise," I echoed what my dad had said without thinking. Elaine glared at me angrily and turned away. I wished I had bit my tongue.

Bud and Cynthia had their heads so close together that I couldn't tell where his brown hair ended and her strawberry blond hair began. But in a minute, Bob Stewart picked his way to the front, tapping Bud as he passed. Bud got up and followed him.

The cheerleaders didn't come over our way very often, so sometimes the band members led cheers. Tonight, Bob and Bud stood in front of our bleachers and yelled, "Gimme an *M!*"

We shouted "*M!*"

"Gimme an *I!*"

"*I!*" and on through the name Middlebrook. Then Bud yelled, "All right, let's do it backward! Gimme a *K!*"

"*K!*" we all answered.

"Gimme an *O!*"

"*O!*" everyone yelled.

Everyone was laughing by the time we got to "And what do you have?"

"Koorbelddim!"

I thought Bud was so clever, until he went back to sit with Cynthia again. I turned to Elaine and realized that she had moved down the row to sit directly in front of Ryan. They were talking, and Elaine's eyes flashed with excitement.

It seemed like no time before we were lining up for the halftime show. We stuck to easy music for this first game, which featured a back-to-school theme. It was a thrill being out there in the bright lights, knowing that everyone was watching for what we would do next. We played *School Days*, a salute to visiting Winston High School, and *The Flintstones* cartoon theme. Then we played our alma mater, *Oh, Middlebrook*, and marched off the field with the fight song.

"Good show," Mr. Cavatina commented as we returned to the bleachers. "Go get a snack, but I want everyone back here by the fourth quarter."

I was dying for a drink and headed for the refreshment stand—alone again. I supposed that Elaine had gone off with Ryan. "I'll have one lemonade, please," I told Mr. Saunders. The band parents run the refreshment stand, and I know Todd's father, because they live down the street from me.

"Ginger!" I heard, and looked around. I almost dropped my drink when I realized Joel was hurrying toward me.

"Hi! Do you want to take a walk for a few minutes?" he asked. He fell into step beside me, and we walked away from the crowd, circling the track. I offered him part of my drink, and I hoped that Elaine wouldn't see us talking together.

"Thanks," he said as he handed back the drink. "That's what I wanted to say, anyway. Thanks for letting me borrow Horatio."

I smiled at him. Nobody else calls my saxophone by name. "Well?" I asked. "How did it go?"

He grinned. "Pretty well, I guess. They let me in. I'll get a rental sax on Tuesday. I'm still trying to remember the fingerings, but I'll get the hang of it soon."

I stared at him. "You mean you don't know how to play the saxophone, and you tried out for the jazz band on it?"

He misunderstood. "Gee, I guess you're mad because I used your sax, and I had never played before. I really was careful with it."

I shook my head. "No, it's okay. But how did you do that?"

He shrugged. "Well, I figured I'd be better off trying out on sax, because it's a reed instrument like the clarinet. I wouldn't have made it on trumpet."

I laughed at that, and then shook my head. "I don't know. If Mr. Cavatina will let you into his precious jazz band on a sax you've never played, you might as well try anything."

He cocked his head and looked at me from under long, thick eyelashes. "I might just do that, Ginger. Try anything, I mean."

I didn't know how he meant that, especially with the look he gave me. It made me nervous. "Uh, yeah," I said. "I have to go. I'll see you later." I couldn't wait to get back to the bleachers.

How could he have made the jazz band? I wondered. It is almost a professional group. The whole band even goes to a special music clinic each summer. Maybe I was right in the first place. Maybe he *was* blackmailing someone.

I looked back toward where I had left him, but another girl was talking with him now. It was a blond sophomore who plays the trumpet. Obviously, Joel didn't remain alone for long.

I was going to tell Elaine about Joel getting into the jazz band, but she was sitting with Ryan. They were "not watching the game" together. I don't think she even missed me.

Six

M ONDAY was one of those foggy, autumn-like mornings. Mist swirled around our feet, and my hair uncurled as we stood on the practice field. We had new music and new field positions to learn.

I was not happy to begin the week, thanks to a long, dull weekend. Elaine forgot all about the shopping trip we had planned, and she didn't answer my phone calls. The only thing that was halfway fun was when Joel called to ask if he could borrow Horatio for jazz band practice on Monday and Tuesday.

Joel told me that next week's show would include The Beach Boy's song, *I Get Around*. I wondered how he could know about the band show ahead of time. He seemed to know all sorts of things about Mr. Cavatina's plans that nobody else knew.

The show was complicated. We were to use

it this week when we went to Northbrook High, and again next week for homecoming. We stepped off into diamond patterns, moved back together into a block, and then marched out into diamonds in the other direction and back again.

I didn't notice that Joel was walking next to me as we went into the band room. But as Elaine moved away, I felt him looking at me.

"Thanks a lot for letting me borrow your saxophone, Horatio, Ginger."

"It's no problem," I said. "He hasn't objected to you."

Joel smiled. "He's a good instrument. How do you like the music this week?"

"It's nice," I said. Then I saw Bud walking alone. I stepped up my pace. Maybe I could catch up to him. But I was too late, because he turned the corner, and Cynthia was there waiting for him. She looked cute, as always. *Rats!* I thought. *Why couldn't I have just one chance to talk with Bud?*

* * * * *

"What's that all about?" Elaine demanded later as we started toward physical science class.

"What's what all about?"

"You know, you and the know-it-all, Joel." She spat out his name as if it tasted bad to say it.

"It's nothing. He's borrowing Horatio until he gets a rental sax for jazz band."

"He's borrowing it again? Isn't that awfully generous of you, Ginger?" She curled her hair around her finger, and I knew something was bothering her.

"Come on, Elaine. It's only for a day or so. He knows how to take care of it. What's wrong with that?"

She sniffed. "You might have to disinfect it," she said.

"Uh-huh," I said as I tuned her out. I had just seen something very interesting. Outside the science room, I caught a glimpse of a peach sweater. I turned around just in time to see Cynthia walking down the hallway with Norm Carter, the tall, blond, senior football captain.

She and Norm were so close that I wished Bud would appear to see them, but he didn't. I thought that perhaps Cynthia had broken it off with Bud. I couldn't help smiling. Maybe I'd have time to reapply my makeup before I went to my locker after school. *Bud's locker is practically next to mine!*

The rest of the day was dull, except that

in English class, I told Paul Sproul that I enjoyed watching his run Friday night. He thanked me with an embarrassed grin. His red face made all the freckles stand out under his red hair.

"...paragraph about a special memory that you have," Mrs. Jamison was saying. "Make it creative. I want to see, feel, taste, and smell your memory. I want to hear what you heard, and know what it was like to be there."

Normally, Mrs. Jamison's class is interesting. But, today, all I could think about was Cynthia walking close to Norm. I did think about senses, though. I thought about the clean smell of Bud's after-shave, and the sound of his voice.

I didn't see Bud after school, or Cynthia either. I wondered if I took too long in the rest room combing my hair and putting on my lipstick. But as I stood by my locker, I heard "Ginger?" It wasn't the voice I was hoping for.

"Uh, hi," I said.

Something about Joel looked unusual. He seemed less arrogant, less sure of himself. I couldn't figure out what was different. He was hiding something in his hand, and a thick lock of his black hair was falling over his forehead.

"How was jazz band?" I asked.

"It was fine. Uh, Ginger? I wanted to say thanks, for letting me use your sax. So, I made this for you," he said quickly. Then he grabbed my empty hand and dropped something into it. It was a little plastic box. I opened it, and inside was a brand-new reed.

"Gee, you didn't have to do that. What? You made it?" I looked up. His eyes were very wide and very blue.

"Joel," I said in my best schoolteacher voice. "Reeds are made from trees, bamboo trees. Didn't you ever hear the poem? *Only God can make a tree.*"

He grinned. "Well, I help Him out a little in my spare time," he said. Although it was another arrogant statement, for once I didn't feel angry.

"What I mean is," he continued seriously, "I bought a hard reed, and shaved and sanded it. So, it should be just about right for you."

It was a generous gesture, and I knew it. Machine-cut reeds are not always even. But I had never heard of anyone sanding his own. "How long did it take you to make it?"

"Just a couple hours, I guess," he answered uneasily.

He spent that much time to make this reed for me, just because I had loaned him my sax. I felt ashamed for not being very nice to him.

"Thank you, Joel. I know it will be a good reed."

He took a breath. "And there's something else. Would you go to the Homecoming Dance with me?"

If my face didn't look totally numb, my hands acted on it. I let go of my books, and they crashed into a heap at our feet.

Seven

I turned all of my attention to the books at our feet, so Joel couldn't see the confusion on my face.

"Oh, I'm sorry! Did they hit you?" I chattered. "I don't know why I get so clumsy sometimes."

Joel bent down and helped me pick them up. The whole time I just kept thinking, *What would Elaine say if I went to the dance with Joel? And what were my chances that Bud would ask me?* I really did want to go—and not with a bunch of girls. I finally ran out of other things to look at besides Joel. He was staring at me, waiting for my answer.

I wanted to crack a joke, but that would tip him off that I was nervous. I crammed my books in the locker and slammed the door. Then I leaned against the locker, took a deep breath, and said, "Yes, I would like to go to the dance with you."

"Great!" he said with a grin. Right then I knew where I had seen eyes that sparkle like Joel's do. My dad's do the same thing when he laughs. "I've got to get home," Joel said. "I've got a lesson at 4:30. I'll call you tonight, okay?"

I walked home slowly banging Horatio against my legs. My thoughts were all mixed-up. They went back and forth between *Wow! I've got a date for homecoming,* and *Elaine sure is going to be mad when she hears about this.* Then I wondered why he asked *me,* anyway. Was it because he didn't know anyone else to ask, or because I had loaned him my saxophone?

I reminded myself that homecoming was only two weeks away. If I was lucky, maybe I could keep the news from Elaine until the last minute.

I walked into the house and yelled, "Mom! Guess what? I have some great news. I have a date for homecoming." I left Horatio in the living room and hurried out to the kitchen. Elaine was shoving golden brown cookies off a tray with a spatula, while Mom dropped spoonfuls of dough onto other trays.

"Ginger, that's terrific!" Elaine beamed. "Is it Bud? How did you talk him into it?"

"That's wonderful, honey. Do I know him?" Mom asked. I just kept staring at Elaine. Finally, I said, "What are you doing here?"

She smiled. "Sorry I didn't walk with you. My mom is at the board meeting at school, and I stopped to see her. I thought you'd left already, so I just came over here to wait for you. She'll pick me up on her way home. But, come on, tell me how you got Bud to ask you to the dance."

"It's not Bud," I started, then gulped. This was not the way that I wanted to tell her. "It's um—" I turned to Mom. "It's Joel Stockwood, Mom. He's new this year."

I heard a sharp intake of breath behind me, but I didn't dare turn around. My mother stuck the cookie sheet into the oven and took out three glasses for milk. I hurried to pour the milk, and we sat down. When my eyes met Elaine's, I was surprised that she didn't look angry or anything. She was just staring.

Mom filled in the conversation. "Well, I have to be a typical mother. Who is he? Where does he live? Who are his parents? And what do they do?" she teased.

"Oh, Mom, I don't know much about him yet." I tried to smile, but my mouth seemed to get stuck halfway. I avoided looking at Elaine again.

Mom smiled, and her eyes twinkled behind her glasses. Mom has pretty, ginger-colored hair that is short and curled around her face. She has quite a few gray hairs, too, but on her it doesn't look bad. "I presume he's in the band," she said.

"He plays the clarinet," Elaine said in a hard, clipped tone.

"He also plays the saxophone in the jazz band," I added.

"There's my mother," Elaine interrupted, pushing her chair back. "I have to go. Thanks a lot, Mrs. Pockel."

She grabbed her books and raced out the door as I yelled, "I'll call you!"

"What's the matter?" Mom asked in surprise.

"Oh, Elaine doesn't like him," I said. It was the world's biggest understatement.

*   *   *   *   *

"You're selling yourself short," Elaine said over the telephone that evening.

"Going to homecoming doesn't mean that I'm joining an enemy camp or anything," I said in defense. "I just happen to want to go, and he's the one who asked me."

"Yeah, well, you still have almost two weeks

until the dance. What if somebody more interesting asks you to the dance?" Elaine protested. "What if Bud asks you?"

"There isn't any chance of that happening," I assured her. "But maybe seeing me at the dance will convince Bud that I'm datable."

"Yeah, you can always look over Joel's head while you're dancing to see who else is available."

"Stop that, Elaine. I don't think Joel is so bad."

Talking with Elaine about Joel was impossible. I've never heard her be so irrational. Her reaction to him was something entirely beyond my understanding. I realized that it was going to be a long two weeks.

Eight

FRIDAY night when we were at Northbrook High, Mr. Cavatina made us sit by sections. He said he wanted a "cohesive sound" when we played for touchdowns. I thought that there wasn't much chance of it tonight. Northbrook has won the city football, basketball, and baseball championships for at least a dozen years.

But I wasn't sorry to sit just two places away from Bud. It also got me out of sitting with either Joel or Elaine during the game. With Joel, I'd worry about what to say, and with Elaine, I'd have to listen to her nasty remarks about Joel.

Elaine said that Joel and I couldn't have anything in common. She warned that if anybody else asked me to the dance, I should grab him instead. She was making me worry about whether Joel and I really would have anything to talk about.

The only exciting thing about the first half was that Paul Sproul made the first touchdown. Nobody expected our school to score at all, so everyone got excited and yelled a lot. We played the fight song twice. Bud grabbed both Bill and me at once and hugged us all together. *That was wonderful.* But then we all sat down, and Bud didn't look at me for the rest of the half.

The halftime show went pretty well, and Mr. Cavatina seemed pleased with us. When we went to get refreshments, Joel caught up with me. "Come on, Ginger. I want you to meet some people."

We walked over to where the home team's band sat, and Joel stopped a tall boy with curly, brown hair, thick glasses, and an alto sax. "Ginger Pockel, this is my friend Walter Vanderbosh," Joel said formally. "Don't be fooled by the saxophone, Ginger. Walt is really a pianist."

Walter pumped my hand cheerfully. "It's a pleasure, Ginger. Joel, how do you do it? You just got to Middlebrook, and you've snatched up the prettiest girl already. How is Middlebrook? Did you get into the jazz band, or are you still a clarinet purist?"

Walt seemed to plunge from one subject

right on to the next one without ever waiting for an answer. He didn't even give me a chance to blush at his compliment.

"I won't tell. Fine. Yes. And, no," Joel answered, "in that order."

Walt frowned at him, and Joel said, "You'd like it, Walt. Middlebrook has a lot of good musicians."

Walt shrugged. "Band isn't as important for me. Hey, did you hear that the Pittsburgh Symphony is coming?"

"No, but if you'll hum a few bars, maybe I can pick it up," Joel said.

"I mean it. They're giving a concert. But the concert is on a Friday, and we'll probably be marching some place." Walt grimaced at his saxophone. "Are you a musician, Ginger?"

"No, I'm just a saxophonist," I said, and Walt laughed.

"Your band looks good. I can tell that it'll be spectacular by the end of the season," Walt commented.

"It's only fair, isn't it? Your football team always beats ours," I observed.

"Ginger, do you like science fiction?" I never saw anyone change subjects like Walt did. While I was trying to come up with an answer, he shoved a paperback book into my hand. "I just finished this book. See what you think of it, and then give it to Joel when you're done."

I'd never read a science fiction book in my life. This one had a cover that was painted with purple mountains against a green sky. I quietly said "thank you," and stuck the book in my pocket. Walt was one of those people you quickly felt like you had known a long time.

Joel also introduced me to a few other band members from Northbrook, and he introduced me to Mr. Carter, the band director.

"Are you enjoying Middlebrook, Joel?" Mr. Carter asked.

"Yes," Joel said. "You were right about Mr. Cavatina, and it was worth changing schools for the harmony class."

Mr. Carter said, "I could have tutored you, but a class is better. Besides, Ed Cavatina is known as tops in this city."

We spent so much time talking with the Northbrook band people that we were late getting back to our side. As we scrambled into the bleachers, Joel said, "You didn't mind, did you? I just wanted to show you off."

I didn't have an answer to that comment, so I simply said that I liked Walt.

"Walt loves the piano and science fiction," Joel said. "I hope you didn't mind his forcing his newest book on you."

While I was pushing past Bud to get to my seat, I realized that it was easy to talk with Joel and his friends.

Paul Sproul's touchdown was our only excitement in an otherwise Northbrook-dominated game.

* * * * *

"Your styles are stiff and stilted," Ms. Dyer said Monday during journalism class. She shoved a pencil behind her ear and rattled our papers at us. "Not one of you got all five *W*'s into your paper. Reporters, I need to use one of these stories for the school newspaper. I've marked them all. Please correct them, and get them back to me tomorrow."

I looked at the red marks all over my paper. *Journalism wasn't going to be as easy as it looked,* I thought.

"I hope you are making good progress on your feature articles," she reminded us. "Don't forget that they are due next Monday."

I groaned inwardly. *I still didn't have any idea what to write about.*

* * * * *

Elaine continued to insult Joel every chance

she got during the rest of the week of home-coming. She didn't care whether he heard her or not. I wished that Ryan would ask her to the dance, so she'd have something else to talk about.

It seemed odd that I had a date for homecoming and Elaine didn't. If I had been going to the dance with anyone else, I would have thought Elaine was jealous.

Joel either pretended that he didn't hear her remarks, or else he didn't catch them. I wasn't sure if I felt bad for Joel, or simply disgust because he put up with Elaine's wisecracks.

On Tuesday, Mom and I went shopping. I got a gorgeous, peach dress with a wide skirt that was trimmed in ribbons and lace. Mom marked the hem, and I spent two evenings shortening it.

Even though I had a date with Joel, I kept remembering Elaine's words about looking around. On Wednesday, I finally got my nerve up to ask Bud how the Debate Club was doing this year in its matches. Ever since the day Bud and Bill almost had me in tears, they had been ignoring me completely.

Bud didn't even look at me. From the corner of his mouth he said, "The answer is alternative energy sources. The question is nuclear power—yes or no."

"Are you for or against it?" I asked.

His mouth curled into a grimace of disgust. He sounded like he thought I couldn't possibly be more stupid. "In debate, Pockel, you're prepared to argue either side. What you believe doesn't matter. What matters is how you present the arguments."

"Do you mean that you don't know which side you're taking? Or, do you mean that you don't care?" I asked sarcastically.

He raised one eyebrow and said, "I'm affirmative." Then he turned to Brian and asked, "Did you hear about the two boy silkworms pursuing the girl silkworm? They ended up in a tie."

I couldn't help it. I giggled. But Brian wrinkled his nose, and Bud frowned at me. His look said that I irritated him, but I had no idea why.

Nine

THE Friday of homecoming finally arrived. The night was filled with a darker sky and crisper air than I'd ever seen before. And the lights illuminated the stadium so brightly that I thought it could be seen from any place. I didn't want to miss a minute of this evening, despite Elaine's repeated warnings that I was going to have an awful time.

The crowd applauded for us at halftime. I could see the colors of their jackets and coats, and the tiny details of the girls' corsages. Even the blue color of the players' uniforms seemed brighter than usual.

Middlebrook never wins all the games like Northbrook, and never loses all of them like Winston. But I had the feeling that if I cheered for our team, it might make a difference. That night, the teams took turns having the lead. I forgot to be mature like Elaine, and I cheered with all my might.

Rockybrook was two points ahead with only a minute left to play. It looked like it was all over. Then Paul Sproul caught a pass and ran practically the whole length of the field for a touchdown in the last seconds. And so we won our homecoming football game. We all cheered and played the fight song while we tried to jump up and down. Even Bud joined in the fun.

I didn't see Joel at all during the game. He was there, sitting hunched over and looking alone in his assigned seat next to Elaine. But when we went to get snacks, he disappeared. I took my orange drink and walked around with Elaine. She was going to the dance with a group of girls, and hoping Ryan would be there. I wondered if Bud was going with Cynthia until he asked, "Are you going to the dance, Pockel?"

"Sure," I said, hoping I sounded cool. My stomach started its own aerobic dance against my ribs. Would he ask me for a dance? Would he have asked me if I said I wasn't going? I hoped he would ask who I was going with, but he didn't. Instead, he turned to Brian, and suggested that they take a look around the place. So, he wasn't going to the dance with Cynthia, after all.

I was excited that Bud would see me in my new dress. Maybe then he would realize that I could be a great date. I just knew this was going to be a terrific evening. I hurried to put my sax away and pull my dress from my locker. Band members always change in the rest room. But when I walked in, the mixture of makeup and perfume mist practically drowned me.

Elaine was busy straightening out her soft gray dress. It was tailored with a white collar and a red belt, and it looked just right for her. "Is Joel's dad driving you home from the dance?" she asked me while we brushed our hair and bobbed around elbows to see the mirror.

"Oh, we're walking home," I told her. "I only live two blocks away, you know."

Elaine rolled her eyes in exasperation. "Oh, brother! He can't even get someone to drive you home? I suppose he thinks the honor of going to the dance with him will impress you enough by itself." She curled her finger around her hair, and I wished that I had lied. "Oh, well, Ginger, you can always join Georgette and Janice and me if you're bored out of your skull." She moved over to the corner of the mirror to check her hair.

I hoped that being with Joel wouldn't be

that bad. Looking at the roomful of giggling girls, I almost wished I were joining Elaine and the others. Then I remembered that having a date for homecoming had been my big dream, so I hurried to finish my hair and left.

Joel was waiting by my locker, wearing a dark suit and a wide smile. He looked different, taller. He handed me one of the Student Council's corsages, a white mum surrounded by blue and white ribbons. Nothing could have made me happier than that corsage. I pinned it onto my dress, and we went into the gym.

What a surprise! Middlebrook's gym looked great. Tonight, the Student Council had hidden the rafters in an umbrella of blue and white, crepe-paper streamers. The lights were dimmed, and several small tables were covered with white and blue paper. Each table had a tiny, glitter-covered football as the centerpiece.

"Tim's saving us a table," Joel said. He steered me down the stairs and across the floor to Tim Brown and Judy Wilson, both sophomore trumpet players. Judy had changed from her usual boyish look to a bright blue dress. Tim went to change from his uniform. I watched Judy follow his progress across the gym.

I didn't know Judy very well. I thought I ought to say something. I tried, "How do you like band, Judy?"

"Excuse me?" She gave me a puzzled look, as if I had pulled her away from her thoughts. "I like it all right. But I'm not great at working that hard."

"Do you want to dance, Ginger?" Joel interrupted. Automatically, I stood up. I hoped that Judy didn't mind, but I couldn't think of what else to say to her.

Then Joel put his arms around me. I stared into those strange, deep blue eyes, and something weird happened. I couldn't feel the floor beneath me. Joel was a great dancer. My feet always turn into bricks on a dance floor, but that night they turned into feathers.

He must have guided the conversation, too. Because the next thing I knew, I was telling him about my parents, my favorite adventure novels, and even how I felt about band. "It's one thing I do that my parents don't know anything about and haven't done before," I said. "It's all mine."

That sounds like serious talk, but it really wasn't, because we were laughing and joking the whole time we were talking. Joel's jokes were mostly bad puns, but I've always been a sucker for a bad pun.

We danced and danced. We did fast dances that I never thought I could do, and slow ones, too. I never once was bored. When the band took a break, I was sorry to have to quit dancing. Joel led me to the bandstand.

"Hey, Don!" Joel called. "Ginger, I'd like you to meet Don Warner."

Up close, Don was tall and skinny. The elevated bandstand made him look like a radio antenna, but he folded over his long body to shake hands and said, "I'm glad to meet you, Ginger," and then he turned to Joel.

"What are you doing down there, Stockwood? You could be doing this."

Joel shrugged. "I've got to enjoy myself sometimes, Don." Joel turned to me. "Don is majoring in music education. He pays his way through school by playing the guitar at some of the clubs around town. At the university, he plays the violin. It takes a lot of guts to play string instruments, you know."

Don winced. "That's very funny, Stockwood."

After we went back and the music started, I asked Joel how he had met them.

"Don went to Northbrook last year, and I've played with them a few times when they needed someone to fill in on electric guitar."

"You went from the guitar to the saxophone?" I asked, amazed at the range of his ability.

"I wanted to learn to play the saxophone while I was here. It seemed to be such a fascinating instrument."

Just then I saw Bud and Brian come into the gym. Without thinking, I quickly scanned the room for Cynthia. She and Norm Carter were locked together in a slow dance. Her pink dress shimmered like silk as they danced. Bud was staring at Cynthia, too, and the next dance I noticed that she was in his arms.

Joel gulped down his punch. "Come on, Ginger," he said, "let's dance again."

Sometime during the evening, I noticed Elaine dancing with Ryan, but she ignored us.

I had to admit that I was sorry to see the dance end. I guess the others were, too, because we all decided to walk to Cyndy's Soda Shoppe afterward.

Cyndy's was alive with chatter about the dance. Several people had come from the dance, including Elaine and Ryan. Elaine even stopped to speak to us. Well, she spoke to me, anyway, before she hurried back to their table.

Over my ice cream soda, I asked Tim if he planned to join the jazz band. "Not this year," he answered, shaking his head. "There are too many junior and senior trumpet players. I won't have a chance until next year. I'm not like Joel here, who practices six hours a day."

"You're crazy, Tim," I said. "Nobody in his right mind spends that much of his life on music."

Joel gave me an embarrassed nod, and his ears turned red. He said, "It's not quite six hours," in a voice softer than usual. "Besides, it doesn't seem like practice to me."

I giggled, but my voice sounded strange. "Joel's already great. He doesn't need to work at it, right?" I asked jokingly. I hoped it sounded like a joke. But there was something odd about the whole thing.

Ten

I woke up Saturday with my mind still in a haze. The mum from the night before seemed to beam at me from its vase on my nightstand.

After the dance, I lay awake in bed for a long time thinking about the dance. I enjoyed being with Joel and giggling at the jokes of the musicians who crowded around our table. But then I remembered the change in the atmosphere when we were at Cyndy's. I shivered and sat up.

I was still sitting in bed when I heard the telephone ring and Dad call me to pick up the extension. It was Elaine.

"Well, did you have fun?" I asked her before she had a chance to ask me.

"Yes, it was so much fun, Ginger. We had the best time. You aren't mad that we didn't walk home with you, are you?"

"No, Joel walked me home," I replied.

"I figured you would be so bored that you probably couldn't wait to get home."

I felt uncomfortable with Elaine talking like that, even though Joel and I had only gone out once. But it's awfully hard to disagree with Elaine. I said, "Listen, Elaine," but that's as far as I got.

She had already dismissed the subject of Joel, and had gone on to the subject of Ryan.

"I'm glad you got together with him, Elaine. But right now I'm standing here in my night-gown, freezing."

"What? You never sleep in, Ginger!" She stopped for a moment, and then she said, "Oh, well, I suppose it wore you out listening to Joel's one-man fan club. I just wanted to tell you that I can't go to the movies with you tonight. Ryan asked me to go with him. Now I've just got to find something to wear."

"Congratulations, Elaine," I said. "Don't worry about the movies. I've got so much homework that I probably won't be going anywhere for the rest of the weekend."

I shuddered, remembering the journalism paper that was due. I never did interview a teacher. I couldn't think of an exciting subject, let alone an exciting teacher.

I dressed hurriedly. But instead of doing

my homework, I cleaned up the top three layers of junk in my room, helped Mom bake some cookies, practiced the music for next week, and wondered why I couldn't forget about last night.

When Joel called at about 3:00, I still hadn't geared up to do schoolwork.

"Hi!" he said brightly. "What would you say to a bike ride?"

"Hello, bike ride," I said automatically, and then I clapped my hand over my mouth.

"That's cute," he groaned. "I'll be right over." *Rats!* I thought. *I didn't mean to encourage Joel.*

He arrived on an old, fenderless bicycle. "Isn't this great? I got it at the police auction," Joel said as we took off for the bike trail in the park. "It doesn't look like much, but it's a 10-speed."

We were pedaling slowly, side by side. "Did you practice six hours today?" I asked.

He didn't answer. Instead, he looked up and said, "I'll race you to the drinking fountain." Then he was gone.

I couldn't catch up to him, although I got closer than I thought I would. When I got to the fountain, he was stretched out in the grass next to his bike with his eyes closed. I got a drink and sat down.

He rolled to his side and propped his head on his hand, looking at me. Suddenly he was very serious.

"Do you think I'm really weird, Ginger?"

I gulped guiltily. "What do you mean?"

He stared at me, and then he mimicked my words from last night, "Nobody in his right mind would spend that much of his life on music." Suddenly he sat up beside me. I didn't want to look at him, so I looked down, and saw his hands knuckled into fists. That was worse. "Ginger, I do practice a lot. I don't practice six hours every day, maybe, but I do practice a lot."

"Hey, music must be important to you," I said. "But what do I know? It doesn't make any difference what *I* say."

My hand was stretched out on the ground holding me up.

His hand closed over mine. "It makes a difference to me," he said quietly.

I gulped. I didn't know what to say. I didn't want what I said to make a difference to him. A little knot twisted in my stomach.

Abruptly, Joel let go of my hand and wrapped his arms around his knees. He stared out across the field toward the woods where the river wound lazily through the trees. He was quiet for a few minutes. When he began to speak, his voice was distant.

"I've been playing musical instruments since I can remember. I can't tell you when I started playing the clarinet, or when I knew it was the most important thing in my life. But by the time I was in third grade, my parents did without certain things to make sure that I had the best teachers."

I shivered slightly, and hugged my own knees. There was something too personal in his voice. It was like looking into somebody's private diary. He was opening it up for me, but I didn't want the responsibility of reading it. I would have stopped him, but I didn't know how to.

"Even when my folks broke up, and Mom had every reason to pull me out of music, she didn't. You know, my dad is a musician. He's with the Philadelphia Symphony now. But there were all those years when he played anywhere, any way that he could—in bars, at dances, and in clubs until all hours. He didn't make much money, and it was hard for Mom. I think it was the hours, though, that Mom couldn't stand. Or, maybe she just understood that Dad had to go off to try for the big time."

He stopped talking for a minute, and then he continued. "Anyway, Barney's my dad now, and I couldn't ask for a better one. But he resents the time I spend on practicing. He doesn't say much about it. He pays for my lessons, but he's just not interested in music."

Joel turned to look at me. "This is a long way to get to what I wanted to say. Ginger, I can't explain how I feel about music. And I feel this about all music—not just classical, or jazz, or rock, but every kind of music. Someday, I want to write the tunes that are in my head and orchestrate them. That's why I came to Middlebrook.

"I spoke to my dad about it a few months ago. If I am good, he can get me an interview and a tryout at one of the top music schools. But I really have to be good to stand a chance. So, that's why I practice so much. Some people are 30 years old, and they don't know what to do with their lives. But I know what I want, and if I work hard enough, I might get it. Can you understand that?"

Boy, did I have a big mouth. I felt terrible for what I had said the night before. Then I said, "Sure, I understand, Joel. But it shouldn't matter to you what I think, or if anyone understands your music. You're building your *own* dream. Don't worry about what other people think."

He touched me under the chin and grinned,

and then he stood to help me up. "You're right," he agreed. "But it's easier if somebody does understand, especially somebody you like."

That made me uncomfortable. I didn't want to get involved —with Joel of all people. *Elaine would never forgive me. Why had I come today? Why hadn't I made up some excuse?*

"There's a chamber orchestra concert at the university tomorrow afternoon," Joel was saying. "I can get Mom to drive us. Do you want to come? We'll probably have to take my sister and brother, but...."

"Uh, no, I can't," I stammered. "I mean, I have this huge stack of homework, and it's due on Monday. I'll probably have to work all day tomorrow on it." It was true, of course. *So why did I feel so guilty saying it?*

"That's a shame," Joel said. I wasn't sure whether he was answering my words or my thoughts. "I really wanted you to come, because it's *my* kind of music."

"You just told me all music was *your* kind of music."

He grinned. "It is, but I especially like the symphony. It's classical music, I guess you would say."

I must have wrinkled my nose, because he

laughed and said, "You ought to give it a try, Ginger. It's not as boring as it sounds." He picked up the bikes. "Let's stop at my house for a few minutes, okay? I want you to meet my mom."

* * * * *

"So, if you're interested in classical music, what are you doing in marching band and jazz band?" I asked him over a snack in his kitchen.

"I also said all music," he replied, and his eyes twinkled. "Everything from German, beer-hall polkas, acid rock, 30's band music— all of it. Listening to everything can only help make me a better musician."

Then he stared at me in that way he has, as if those blue eyes could probe my thoughts. I flinched, but I didn't turn away, and he smiled. "This marching band is special," he said. "Everyone works so hard, and Mr. Cavatina makes something as small as a halftime show seem so important. I wouldn't miss it for anything. That's what I was trying to tell you that day at school when you got so mad at me."

"Hello!" shouted a cheerful voice. A woman kicked the door open, and walked in with a bag of groceries in each arm. One of the bags was falling, and Joel jumped up to help her.

"Mom, this is Ginger," he said as he placed a sack on the counter. "Ginger, this is my mom, Mrs. Runyon."

Right away, she took my hand and said, "I'm very glad to meet you, Ginger." The warmth in her voice said that she meant it. In the next minute, two children came screeching in, both blond-haired and about four feet tall. The girl grabbed Joel around the waist, shouting, "Save me! Save me, Joel!"

The boy who chased after her with a rolled-up comic book skidded to a halt in front of me and smiled shyly.

"These are the twins," Joel said, as he tried to pull the girl's arms away. "Ginger, meet Jennifer and Jonathan."

Jennifer stared at me boldly with her hazel eyes. Then she immediately dismissed me as unimportant. Her hair was very blond, and it was pulled into a ponytail that reached halfway down her back. When I said, "Hello, Jennifer," she just ignored me.

Then she asked, "Play with me, Joel? Play me a game of *Sorry?*"

But Joel smiled and said, "Not now, Jen." She gave me an angry look, and then she raced off to the living room.

Jonathan smiled at me and stuck out his

hand seriously. "I'm in third grade," he announced, "and I have a new bicycle. Do you want to see it?"

"I'll look at it just for a moment," I said. "Because I've got to get home."

"Won't you stay for supper?" Mrs. Runyan asked. She turned to Joel. "You could put Ginger's bike in the car, and I'll drive her home later."

Joel looked at me, but I shook my head. "I'm sorry. I really need to get home."

"We'll do it another time, then," Mrs. Runyan said and smiled warmly.

I admired Jonathan's new bicycle, which was a great deal better-looking than Joel's bike. Then Joel and I rode back through the park together. I told Joel that I thought the twins were cute.

"You just say that because you don't live with them," Joel chuckled. And then he added, "They're okay, but they want me to play all the time. I mean, *all* the time. Are you sure you can't go with us tomorrow?"

I almost said yes, but just in time, I remembered that I didn't want to get involved.

Eleven

"WHERE have you been all day?" Elaine's voice crackled over the phone. She was talking with Mom when I got home, so I figured she already knew.

"I took a bike ride with Joel," I told her in my best go-ahead-and-make-something-of-it voice.

"Well, if you want to continue seeing a jerk, that's your business. I thought you might go shopping with me."

I was not in the mood to listen to Elaine's anti-Joel campaign. But I didn't have to worry. She went right on.

"I wanted to show you a sweater at McRaftrees. But Ryan is picking me up at seven, and I have to eat first. So, how about Monday instead?"

"Sure," I said, feeling relieved.

Now, to that homework, I thought. But I

still couldn't think of what to write about. *How about English? No, that was too dull. How about journalism? No, Ms. Dyre would think I was trying to be cute.* I went to stare at the TV instead.

I woke after midnight from a restless sleep. I couldn't think of what had woken me up. Then the answer came to me. *I'd write about band.* What a relief. Then I fell asleep.

I woke up early the next morning and got ready to go to church. After we got home, we all were starved, so I helped Mom mix up a batch of French toast. Dad sat at the kitchen table, working on the crossword puzzle.

"What are you doing today, Ginger?" Mom asked.

"Homework," I groaned between mouthfuls. "I've got to write about my favorite school subject for journalism class."

That made Dad look up. He folded his paper and set it aside. "What are you writing about?" he asked. Dad always took notice whenever I mentioned journalism.

"I'm going to write about band," I said. "I was so worried about it, and the perfect subject was staring me right in the face. I'm the only band member in journalism class, so I won't have any competition for the subject."

"Is band your favorite subject?" Mother

asked frowning at me.

I shrugged. "It's definitely the most fun. Anyway, what can you say about math or science, or English? One kid said he didn't even have a favorite subject, so Ms. Dyre told him to interview the janitor. I think she wants to see how we write the story more than what subject we write about."

I helped with the dishes, and then I went to my room to work on my paper. There wasn't any hope for it. The only way to write was to write. I wrote three pages of beginnings and crossed out each one. Then I decided to write the middle and spread out from there.

I described Mr. Cavatina, right down to his favorite expressions like, "If there were a blade of grass an inch high, you'd trip over it." I wrote about lines and formations, and about memorizing music every week. Then I stopped again. I couldn't think of anything else, but I knew it wasn't enough. I looked out the window, beyond my street, past the housetops, to the trees that marked the park where we had biked yesterday. That's what I wanted! I wanted the enthusiasm that Joel had when he talked about music.

I tried to remember what Joel had said. I quoted his description of how the band was a family when we worked so hard together. I described the nervousness of Friday evenings, the smell of the brass polish, the cold metal under our hands, and the lights on the field.

When I started to type the story, I had to turn on a light. It was getting dark. It didn't seem as though I had been writing that long, but then I noticed that my legs were cramped. It was 6:00. My mind did one of those odd double takes. For no reason, I thought of Joel practicing for six hours.

*   *   *   *   *

Monday morning I combed my hair for the fourth time. *You're really crazy, Ginger,* I told myself. As soon as you get outside, your hair will blow everywhere. I wore my good green skirt and checked my makeup again. Maybe I thought Bud would look at me differently now, after the dance.

I wondered whether I would have to put Joel off, or whether refusing the concert had been enough. His practicing would keep him busy enough. And Elaine's remarks had made last week miserable enough for a lifetime.

I decided to try to forget about Joel. He was so serious about his career that he surely wouldn't miss me. And I wanted to see if I could get Bud to notice me.

Twelve

WORDS are fickle. It seems like great words join themselves together in my mind, but when the time comes to use them, the words disappear.

That's the way I felt when I met Bud that morning in the hall. I needed cue cards printed on my shoes just to ask him if he enjoyed the Homecoming Dance.

"It was okay, if you like that sort of thing," he said casually. "Do you have this week's music memorized, Pockel?"

He didn't even seem to notice my green skirt, or how spectacular I had looked at the dance Friday. All I got was a reminder that he thought I was irresponsible enough not to know my music. *He made me mad.* "Don't worry about it. I won't embarrass you," I shot at him, a little more angrily than I'd intended.

"Okay, short stuff." He stalked away, and

I bit my lip with fury.

Great job, Ginger, I mumbled to myself. *You finally get his attention, and then you snap at him. You're only mad at yourself for not knowing what to say. Why aren't you witty and warm and wonderful, instead of crabby?* Now it was too late. I got my sax and went outside.

On the frosty practice field, we began rehearsing our new show. Some of us couldn't seem to remember which foot came after which.

It seemed that I didn't need to worry about being pursued by Joel. He smiled at me once from across the band room, but he didn't wait for me after band. Bud wasn't speaking to me either, after my outburst earlier. And Elaine was too busy with Ryan to notice me. When I got to the science room, she was leaning by the door talking with him. She barely managed to float in at the last bell.

At lunch, Elaine tried to describe the movie she and Ryan had seen. But from her description, I gathered she must have spent more time watching Ryan than the screen. "He is so nice," she beamed. "You can't imagine how fun and sweet he is. Do you think he'll ask me to the Winter Fair?"

I shook my head. Elaine was already

scheming. It wasn't even Thanksgiving, and she was thinking about the big Christmas festival and dance.

"Are we still going shopping?" Elaine asked.

"Sure," I said between bites of my sandwich.

"Oh, no, here he comes," Elaine warned suddenly. She looked away, and hurriedly gathered up her lunch. "I'm sorry I can't stay, Ginger, but one period a day is enough to put up with *him*."

"Huh?" I asked, but Elaine was already across the room tossing her lunch into the waste can.

"Where did she go?" Joel's voice was close behind me. I whirled around and knocked over my almost-empty milk carton.

"What happened to Elaine?" he asked again.

"Oh—she—I don't know," I stammered. "I think she had to see someone. Uh, I didn't know you had lunch this period, Joel."

He said, "Usually I go to the band room instead." Then his eyes flickered over me. For a moment I was glad I'd worn green, even if the attention was from Joel and not Bud. "I need to practice jazz band music," he went on, "and I don't like to carry a saxophone home the way you do."

"I don't like to carry it," I told him. "But I'd rather go home and practice than not know the music."

He said, "I wanted to ask if you'd wait for me after school today. I've got something in my locker for you. Okay?"

"Okay, but what..." It was too late. He was gone, and in a minute Elaine reappeared.

"Why did you do that to me?" I demanded.

Elaine smirked. "Well, I knew you two would want to be alone," she said dramatically.

"Stop it. It's embarrassing to have to make excuses for you."

"Then don't," Elaine said angrily. "I don't care if he knows that I can't stand him. What did he want, anyway?"

"He asked me not to leave too fast tonight. He's got something in his locker for me. And Elaine, I wish you'd stop saying mean things about him."

"If you don't care about him, then why should it bother you?" she asked. Without waiting for an answer, she walked off.

I was happy to hand in my journalism paper. It isn't often that I do something I'm very pleased with. By the time I finished it last night, I really was glad that I'd spent the time on it.

After classes, I hung around the lockers for a while. Elaine gave me a sickening-sweet smile and told me she would "let us be alone together." I stood there for a while until I began to feel foolish. I finally slammed the locker door and started down the hall.

"Wait!" Joel called. He came racing out of the band room. "Wait a minute, Ginger." He spun the dial on his lock and opened the locker door. Then he took out a record folder and handed it to me. "Can I talk you into listening to this album?"

I looked at the cover. "Overtures by Rossini?" I questioned. "Who is he?"

"He's one of those weird classical composers," Joel said, and grinned. "Actually, you will probably recognize some of these."

I shrugged. "Well, I guess it won't kill me to listen to it." That reminded me of something, and I opened my locker again to get out Walt's science fiction book. "This didn't, anyway. Tell Walt I enjoyed it."

"You liked it?" Joel sounded like he couldn't believe it. "Maybe I'll have to read it."

"I never thought I'd like that kind of book," I admitted. "But it's a good adventure."

"Then you'll like Rossini," Joel predicted confidently. "It's like an adventure without words. See if I'm right."

Thirteen

"THAT'S nice music," Mom commented as she peeked into my room. In the background, Joel's Rossini record was blaring the *William Tell Overture* while I did my homework. I'd been playing it every night for a week.

"Thanks," I said, and looked up from typing my descriptive paragraph for English class. "It's Joel Stockwood's record. I've got to take it back to him one of these days."

"Ginger, if you'd like some musical variety, you're welcome to try out some of our classical records that are in the cabinet downstairs."

"Thanks. I'll look at them when I finish this paper," I said.

"Is it for journalism?" Mom asked.

"No, this time it's for English."

"How is journalism going? Are you enjoying it? I knew Mom or Dad would be asking me about it sooner or later.

"It's going okay, I guess," I told her, trying to sound like I didn't care much either way.

Journalism really was going better than just okay. Ms. Dyre's class was so inspiring. I was already daydreaming about working on a newspaper, and the bigger stories we'd get to do later in the semester.

But knowing that Mom wanted me to like the class made me not want to admit that I did. One little admission like that, and my whole life would be planned for me.

"It's not as exciting as band?" Mom asked.

"Nothing is, Mom."

The telephone rang, and she went to answer it.

Band and journalism definitely were the best. I thought about the story I'd written about band. The day after we handed them in, Ms. Dyre asked me to stay after class. She held my article in her hand. "Ginger, this is really something," she said.

I didn't know what she meant. I thought I'd been too sappy about the band. There was no grade on it. All the other papers on her desk had been graded.

She said, "This is almost poetry. Nobody who reads this will ever go out for a hot dog during the halftime show."

"Uh, thank you, Ms. Dyre," I said. *How do you respond to a compliment from a teacher?*

"I sent a copy to the state newspaper association's annual feature-writing contest. You don't mind, do you?"

I was flattered, even excited, but I wasn't going to tell my parents about it unless I had to. I didn't want the pressure that they'd put on me then.

"Ginger!" Mom called from downstairs. "The telephone is for you."

"Hi there!" Joel's voice bounded over the line at me.

"You remember Walt, don't you? He just called. He told me that he has two extra tickets to the Pittsburgh Symphony next Friday. Will you go with me?"

"Well, I...."

"We don't have to play in band on that Friday, because there's no school that day. The game is Thursday that week, remember? Walt even said that he hoped you'd come."

I thought of Walt and his science fiction book. "I guess I could go," I said.

"Great! You'll enjoy the concert, Ginger. They're playing Copland, Barber, and the *1812 Overture.*"

The names confused me, but *1812 Overture* sounded familiar to me. I didn't have to say anything, because Joel rattled on.

"You'll love the *1812 Overture*. We have a recording of it performed with cannons, but I think it will be better live."

"I didn't think you could get much tune out of a cannon," I commented. "Or, do they shoot the audience to put it out of its misery?"

"Huh?" Then Joel laughed. "I guess I asked for that. Tschaikovsky wrote cannons into the score *with* the orchestra music, because it was to be played outside to commemorate a battle." He paused. Then he asked, "Ginger?"

"Yes?"

"Didn't you like the record?"

He sounded so serious that I couldn't tease him for long. I said, "Oh, I did get around to listening to it, but I'm afraid I have to say that you were right. I liked it."

Then he sounded so smug that I was sorry I had told him. "I thought you would. You seem the type. What's your favorite, the *Lone Ranger?*"

"No, *The Barber of Seville* was my favorite," I said. But his tone and his words were bothering me. "But what do you mean by 'type'?" I demanded. "I don't like being told that I'm a 'type' of anything."

"Oh, Ginger, don't be so touchy about it," Joel said, half laughing. "Believe me, I'd never try to 'type' you."

There was a long pause. Joel finally said, "I meant that I expected you to like Rossini, because it's exciting music. And you're an exciting person."

What could I say to that? It was hard not to melt on the spot.

"I told you, Ginger, that I love all kinds of music. And I'm glad that you like some of them, too. I play somber music a lot of the time. That's another reason it's nice to be with you. You're always so cheerful and bubbly."

"You make me sound like a bottle of soda pop," I grumbled.

"Yeah, like ginger ale!" he agreed, enthusiastically.

That did it. I really was not in the mood for teasing, and I am especially sensitive to certain things.

"Joel, you don't know *anything*," I stated. "You think you can just go around putting people into little boxes, and they'll shape themselves to fit the box like silly putty!"

"Hey, I meant that as a compliment, you know?"

"Yeah, well, just cut it out, okay?"

Our conversation was pretty stilted after that. I ended it with the excuse that I had to finish my homework.

I couldn't concentrate though, and my mind started to wander. Everyone wanted me to fit neatly in with their ideas. My parents wanted me to be the perfect journalist. Joel wanted me to be cheerful and fun. Elaine wanted me to be cool and sophisticated—and to hate Joel. And Bud—I guessed that Bud wanted me to be meek and stay out of his way.

Well, I decided that I would go to the concert, after all. It would be nice to hear it, and I did like Walt. *Type,* I muttered to myself as I got into bed that night. Joel thought I was so simple. Well, he could stand on his head and spit quarters if he wanted to, because I was not going to bubble!

Fourteen

"GOOD morning, Dad," I said.

"Mmf," he acknowledged from behind the newspaper. "How's school going?"

"Fine." I sat down beside him at the kitchen table. He put down the paper.

"Hey, Ginger, aren't you up and around a bit early?"

"We have early practices this week," I said and yawned for emphasis. "The game is Thursday because of a teachers' conference on Friday. I suddenly realized that I'd been staring at something when he folded the paper and put it away. "Dad, can I see the back of that paper?" There was a headline on the section he had been holding.

"Huh?" He turned the paper over to see. "Sure, but are you joining a lobbyist group or something?"

It was a full-page advertisement sponsored by several organizations in the area that were urging a freeze on the building of nuclear power plants.

"No," I answered, "but the Debate Club is working on this subject. I thought they might be able to use the article in their collection of 'anti' arguments."

Dad's mustache drooped. "Oh, well, it's only a puzzle," he mourned as he tore off the page and handed it to me. The crossword was on the back, surrounded by classified ads. I glanced at the ads, and then one small one in the corner of the page caught my eye.

"Thanks, Dad." I grabbed the page and jumped up as the horn blared from Elaine's mother's car. It's only two blocks to school, but when they offer a ride, I don't refuse. After all, Horatio weighs 20 pounds. I put him on the bathroom scale one night to find out.

I found Bud alone at the locker that he shared with Brian, and I held out the newspaper ad. "What's this?" he asked.

"It was in the morning paper," I said. "I know it's all the negative arguments, but I thought you could practice against what this says."

He squinted at the paper through his glasses. "Okay, but why is there a hole in the page?"

"I wanted to keep an ad that was in that

spot. But you're not missing anything."

"Uh, thanks," Bud said.

"Well, good luck," I added lamely. I backed away, and then I went to get Horatio. *I was making progress. Bud had spoken to me without voicing a single insult.*

This week's band production was a neat riverboat formation to the song, *Proud Mary.* Alternate players who didn't have regular positions set off smoke from the smokestacks, and the side-wheeler turned while the whole formation moved down the field. Well, that's what it was supposed to look like.

We couldn't move exactly in a circle pattern. It had to be oval, because the whole formation had moved since the last step. Mr. Cavatina had put mostly seniors and juniors into the wheel, but I was there, too. He must have assumed that the experienced players would show us how to do it. *He was wrong!* Even while we bumbled around and around, we all knew it would look great if we could get it together.

When we were straggling back to the band room, gloomy with thoughts of extra-early morning practices all this week, Bud came up beside me and murmured, "Come on, you can't be tired yet. You're having lots of fun."

I looked right at Bud, and he was almost

smiling. I had a thrill of pleasure at his attention. In the next minute, though, I heard a syrupy voice behind us. I didn't even have to turn my head to recognize Cynthia's voice, "Oh, Bud, I wonder if you could...."

"You guys were having a *wheel* tough time out on the field," Tim said.

"Maybe we need to be playing *I Get Around* this week," Joel added as he joined us. Any other time I'd have enjoyed the joking around, but I lost interest when Bud dropped back to walk with Cynthia.

If Elaine and I in physical science class were any indication, the whole Middlebrook band was in a rotten mood that day. Science was easy for Elaine, who must have memorized the periodic table. I had trouble remembering the symbols for salt. At least having Elaine as my lab partner has kept me from blowing myself up so far, but who knows for how long? The day we separated hydrogen and oxygen from water, I came very close. And today, I dumped nitric acid on my hand. Elaine was so quick getting my hand under a faucet that I barely felt the burn. But then I looked down and saw a huge brownish-orange stain all across my hand. *Great*, I thought. *I finally got Bud to act as if I'm a human being, and now I look like this.*

Joel stopped by our lunch table on his way to the band room during fifth period. This time I grabbed Elaine and wouldn't let her leave.

"Hi," he said. "Good grief! What happened to your hand?"

I quickly stuck it under the table. "It was just a chemical spill. I don't know whether to wear a bandage or admit that I'm an extra-terrestrial, changing back to my original form."

He grinned. "You've been reading Walt's books again."

Elaine glared at both of us, but I ignored her. "I bought two more, but they weren't as good as the one Walt gave me to read."

"On Friday, he can tell you which ones to get. He'll bore you to death if you get him talking. He'll also tease you, but he doesn't mean anything. Well, I better get going. Bye, Elaine."

She barely acknowledged him. As I watched Joel walk away, I realized he was warning me about Walt's teasing. *I guess I shouldn't be so sensitive about everything.*

Elaine just sat there and pouted. "He's so gross. I don't know how you can stand him. I know he's going to challenge me for my seat as soon as marching band is over. And science fiction—," she wrinkled her nose at me.

"What's that about Friday?" she asked. "I thought you weren't going to date him anymore."

I shrugged. "So what? He invited me to the Pittsburgh Symphony concert, and I want to go." She turned her head away and wouldn't even look at me. I tried something different. "Besides, Elaine, why are you so upset about another challenge? Lots of people challenge you. It's never bothered you before. And it's the seniors who I feel sorry for, because they have to put up with two freshmen in the first-chair positions of the clarinet section. First chair is usually a senior's position, you know."

She didn't say anything else. She sat there, twisting her hair into a tight finger curl, and making me feel like a traitor.

Finally, the day seemed a little brighter when I got to journalism class. "Only one student bothered to ask anyone about the Winter Fair," Ms. Dyre said today. "Everyone else didn't bother to get an interview."

I wondered if I was sticking out like a red flag, even though I did feel a little proud. But then she added, "And that person didn't get enough details.

"Now, everybody stand up! You're all going out, right now. Make an appointment, or get that interview before the end of the period."

We got up and started out.

"Ginger Pockel, please wait a minute," Ms. Dyre added. She handed me a letter. "I thought you'd like to see this before you hear it on the morning announcements tomorrow. Your band article won the contest. You've won a $500 savings bond."

"What? I won? Really?" I stammered. "Me?" I didn't know what to say. Right then, I thought of Joel, because his words had given me so many ideas for the article. If I hadn't gone biking with him that day, I doubt that I would have written the article, let alone won a contest with it.

"It's money that you can use when you get to college," Ms. Dyre was saying. "Are you all right, Ginger?"

"I-I think so," I started to say, and then I sat down quickly, because the room looked funny, and my head was so full of thoughts chasing around after each other. "I just can't believe it."

Ms. Dyre smiled. "I can believe it. You've got talent, Ginger. And it helped that you like the subject. You enjoy band a great deal, don't you?"

"Yes," I tried to answer without grinning, but I couldn't stop my mouth from pulling up. "Marching band is about all I do in the fall.

It has to be, because there's not much time for anything else."

"That's the impression I got from reading your story. Are you planning to major in music?"

"Gosh, no," I said. "There are lots of kids in the band who could, but I have to work hard just to be there."

She smiled. "But you have a good time, huh?"

I nodded, and she went on, "Sometimes I think that amateurs have more fun than the professionals do. It's not crucial for them, so they can relax and enjoy themselves."

I got a mental picture of Joel, and of Elaine not wanting him to challenge her. I said, "But the real musicians don't seem to count the cost of being best. They practice as if they don't want to do anything else."

"Does anything affect you that way, too, Ginger?" she asked.

Although my parents often asked me the same thing, the way Ms. Dyre asked didn't feel like prying.

"Not yet," I admitted. I remembered looking up at my darkened room and realizing that the whole day had gone by while I wrote that article. I pushed the picture aside. Journalism was what my dad wanted for me.

It wasn't what I wanted. I had a sudden fear that Ms. Dyre might begin to sound like my father. I grabbed my books, mumbled something about having to get an interview, and got out before she could say anything else.

Fifteen

TO make our early practices even crummier, the weather turned cold and foggy. And things were even worse in the saxophone section. The atmosphere in the band was almost icy. Bud suddenly became the tyrant of the band room. Nobody could please him. Even Brian couldn't tease him out of his awful mood.

When Bud reached his worst point, I finally said, "Lay off us, Bud. What's the matter? Isn't Cynthia speaking to you?"

He stared at me for a minute. His eyes flickered behind his glasses. "No," he mumbled. "There's a debate today against Findley. They were top in the state last year."

"All right, everybody, let's go outside," Mr. Cavatina said. "Today, we are going to practice until we do it right."

"I don't know what makes him think today

will be any different from every other day,"
I muttered as we got our coats.

During a break, I turned to Bud who was
standing behind me. "Findley isn't the best
in the state *this* year," I said. "All they've
got is last year's reputation."

"That's all *you* know, Pockel. They're good,
really good. They've got this one guy...."

"Yes, but they've got the wrong side," I said.

"What do you mean?" Bud asked.

"Think about it, Bud. Their position is to
weaken the need for nuclear plants, isn't it?
Well, how many nuclear power plants supply
electricity to cities in this country?"

"I've got that figure on a card," Bud
shrugged.

"So, Findley will be suggesting that we turn
out the lights on Broadway, that we go back
to horses and buggies, and that we trust the
Russians and the Arabs to supply all our
power. Findley will be suggesting that we turn
our backs on our own scientific capabilities
when we most need them. What we really
need is to figure out ways to use nuclear
energy *safely*."

He stared at me, and my neck prickled.
Perhaps he was seeing me in a new light.

"Let's try this," Mr. Cavatina interrupted
us. He showed us a new series of steps to

help us round out the bottom of the wheel formation. We all tried it again, and then one more time. And it worked, sort of. We were still a lumpy wheel, but it was much better than before. At least now we could tell who was at the bottom of the wheel. After a few more practices, maybe we'd have it.

After band, I passed Bud in the hallway. *And he actually smiled at me.*

"Are you interested in joining the Debate Team?" he asked.

That was tempting, especially when I thought about working with Bud, but I shook my head. I said, "I'd always remember the arguments on the other side. And I've never been a logical arguer. It's not my style."

We were outside when the morning announcements were made, so I wasn't prepared. In English class, Paul Sproul stood up to usher me to my seat. "The celebrity!" he cried. "Congratulations, Ginger."

I felt the flush creep up to my cheeks, but I was proud, anyway. "Ginger's award is an honor for all of Middlebrook High," my homeroom teacher said. "When the Herald comes out, we'll all have to read the article."

Paul tapped me on the shoulder and whispered, "The band does a great job. We never get to see the show, but we hear you during the game. It really cheers us up, especially if we're losing."

"I should have interviewed you, Paul," I giggled.

* * * * *

"May I carry Horatio for you?" Joel asked after school. I was looking for Bud. I didn't even notice Joel was standing beside me.

"Huh? Oh, sure. That's really nice of you, Joel. Do you know what that thing weighs?"

"Sure. I've got one, remember?"

"Oh, yeah. I'm sorry," I said. "Okay, then let me carry your clarinet."

We walked into the cool sunshine. "Most evenings I'm busy after school," Joel said. "But today I'm free. It seems I ought to do something for the winner."

"Thank you," I said. "Joel, that award should be have been yours. Remember that bike ride we took together? The things you said about music that day gave me the ideas for my paper on band."

"You mean my words are appearing in your prose?" he asked with a grin. "Gee, I can't wait to see it. I haven't even joined the symphony yet, and already I'm being quoted." He lifted his chin high and struck a pose, and his blue eyes twinkled.

"Oh, brother!" I cried. "Maybe I'd better carry my sax. Your head's going to be enough weight for you to carry."

He laughed. "Don't give away the credit, Ginger. You earned that award. Writing is a talent. I knew you were taking journalism, but I didn't know you were a real journalist."

I liked the sound of being called a journalist. *Or, did I? What if I decided not to become a journalist? How was I going to talk my parents out of it, now that I'd won a contest?*

We had milk and cookies in the kitchen, and Joel blurted to my mom the news about the award before I could stop him.

Mom squeezed my shoulders and said, "That's wonderful, honey! I didn't even know you had entered."

I didn't like Joel's spouting off about the award like that. Mom was giving me a funny look, and I didn't want to talk about the contest. So, to change the subject, I said, "Will you play for me, Joel?"

He put his glass down on the table with a little clank, and gave me an odd stare. "You're kidding."

"Why, are you afraid?"

"No, but I don't have anything..."

"Joel Stockwood!" I cried. I was upset about his telling Mom about my award. It made me feel like being pushy. "What do you do for six hours a day, anyway? Or, am I not a good enough audience to appreciate your talent?"

He was supposed to be the terrific musician who could move right into the first-chair position of the clarinet section. I thought all that reluctance sounded fake for somebody as confident as Joel.

His frown deepened. His knuckles wrapped around his glass of milk. "It's nothing like that," he snapped. "I guess I didn't think you'd be interested."

Abruptly, he stood up and went to get his clarinet in the living room. I followed him. "It won't be jazz, you know," he said as he began fitting the pieces together. Then he stood up, tapped me on the shoulder, and pushed me gently toward the couch. "What do you want to hear?"

"Surprise me," I said.

He stood still a moment, as if collecting his thoughts. I got a mental picture of him on a stage with an audience before him instead of just me. Maybe he was seeing the same thing, because he stood straight, as if he was giving a performance.

"This is Mozart. It really should have

accompaniment," he said. It wasn't an apology.

That was the end of any argument between Joel and me that day. Joel put the clarinet to his mouth, and I forgot that I'd ever complained. The room faded away as the music soared. I'd never heard clarinet music like this. Joel sounded like a whole orchestra rolled into one instrument. I didn't know a clarinet could make me want to laugh, cry, and dance all at the same time.

I thought of Elaine for a minute. And suddenly, I knew why she was so upset about a challenge from Joel.

When he stopped playing, I was ashamed for my harsh words and for making him mad. I knew I had to apologize, but I couldn't find the words. I started, "I'm sorry, Joel..."

"It was that bad, huh?" he grinned, teasingly. That smoothed the way. He was back to Joel, the high school kid. But I'd never forget the musician I had just heard.

"No, you know what I mean." I giggled. "I'm sorry for saying what I did about being ashamed to play. And, Joel Stockwood, you knew what that would do to me!"

He couldn't stop grinning. "Well, I hoped it would. Anyway, I think you like Mozart."

"I think so, too." We were standing just

about a foot or two apart. There was something pleasantly tense about that moment. I
thought he might just lean forward and kiss
me. Or, I might just kiss him. Or—abruptly,
he turned away.

"It's the *Clarinet Concerto in A Major*, the
first movement," he said as he began taking
the clarinet apart.

Was I imagining things? Maybe Joel didn't
feel that bit of electricity I felt just then. I
gulped. Suddenly, I remembered that I was
supposed to be interested in Bud. And things
were getting more and more tense between
Elaine and me.

"It's beautiful music," I said.

"I played it in the state solo contest last
year. I don't have this year's music yet."

Joel left right after that. I was still a little
dazed by the music. Maybe I also was confused by the strange feelings inside me. I
didn't like being disloyal to Elaine, and right
now, that's how I felt I was being.

Mom came in from the kitchen and leaned
against the doorway. "He's very good," she
said softly.

"Yes, he is. But I hadn't realized how good."

"Now, tell me about the contest," she
prodded.

"Oh." That brought me back to earth. "Do

you remember the weekend I had to write about a favorite subject, and I finally picked band?"

She nodded. I explained about the bike ride with Joel. "I used his ideas. If it weren't for the things that Joel said, I probably never would've gotten it done," I finished.

In the middle of my explanation, Mom began to frown slightly. Abruptly, she straightened her glasses. I knew she had something on her mind.

"Ginger, I want to talk to you about that band."

"Okay." I shrugged. "What about it?"

"I know it means a lot to you, but I wonder if you should spend so much time at it."

"Mom!" I cried in sudden horror. "You wouldn't make me give it up, would you?"

"No, of course, I wouldn't. But it's a lot of work."

"Sure, it's a lot of work. If you aren't dedicated, you're an alternate. Nobody asks if it's important. We just know that it is. I guess we feel that way because we're a part of something bigger than ourselves."

"Ginger, when I hear someone like Joel play, I think perhaps you don't realize how much talent and dedication it takes to make a career in music."

"Oh, yes, I do," I said. "Joel's really talented, but he also practices six hours a day. Boy, was I wrong about him. I actually wondered who he blackmailed to get that first-chair position in the clarinet section. Did you know that he made the jazz band before he even knew how to play the saxophone? I guess it never occurred to me that anybody at Middlebrook could be that good."

"But, as you said, Ginger, it takes talent."

"I know. So what?" I asked.

She sighed. "I know it's important to you, Ginger, but don't you think you ought to give some careful thought to it before you decide on a career in music?"

"Gosh, Mom, I'm not in that league at all. Elaine could go into music if she wanted to. But I don't think she wants to. For me, band is the best way to enjoy high school. I like music. I like to play and march, and be a part of the band. I couldn't be a musician. I'm not that good."

"Lots of music teachers and band directors aren't such great players," Mother observed. She sounded like she had changed her mind and was trying to talk me into it.

"I know," I said, "but I'm not that dedicated. I don't want to be teaching a bunch of kids how to march in the frost and fog when I'm

40 years old. You really have to love it, like Mr. Cavatina does, to do that."

Mom looked pleased, and relieved. I couldn't get over it. Twice in one day people had asked me if I was going to make a career in music.

I put my arms around Mom and hugged her. "When I know what sort of career I want, I'll tell you all about it," I promised. I think it's great to have parents who worry about you, even when there's nothing for them to worry about.

Sixteen

"GHERKIN, I mean, Pockel!"

Bud stopped me in the hallway. I was balanced on one foot, trying to slip my tennis shoe on without falling over. *In the entire world, is there a more unglamorous position for greeting a boy?* Yes, it was my next one, falling over against the locker. I was trying to hurry. I shoved my foot into the shoe and stood up.

"Yes? How was the debate?" I asked. I wondered if I'd combed my hair, if we were going to be late to band, and if I was dreaming. *Bud was actually seeking me out to speak to me? It was too incredible!*

"It was perfect!" he grinned. His face flushed with pleasure. "We bowled them over. Well, our affirmative team did. The negatives lost." He gulped, and then, as if he couldn't stand not telling me, he added, "We didn't

129

win by much, though."

"Congratulations," I smiled. "Didn't I tell you that you could do it?"

"The other schools will worry about meeting us now," he said. "By the way, thanks."

"Sure, anytime," I said. Then I just stood there smiling. I wished I could think of something else to say.

"Uh, hey, I heard about your award. That's great."

"Thank you," I was feeling happier by the minute. Was this the Bud Brandis I'd been waiting to hear something nice from since middle school? And now he was right here in front of me, beaming down at me. I desperately needed something to say, something witty and wonderful. But I should have known it wouldn't last.

"Bud?" Cynthia asked, flapping her eyelashes, "Could you...."

"Wait a minute," he said over his shoulder, and then he looked down at me. "Pockel, I wondered if..."

"Well, if *you* don't have time for me, Bud, then I'll find someone who does!" Cynthia interrupted. She flounced away down the hall.

Bud spun around like a top someone had wound too tightly, and I never found out what Bud wondered about me. "Cynth! Wait!" Bud called as he hurried after her.

Anger and jealousy muddled around inside me. Then something else took over. *If Bud were my boyfriend*, I thought, *I'd never be that demanding. In fact, if I were Bud, I wouldn't let anyone be that demanding of me. I wouldn't put up with it. Why did Bud put up with her?*

I didn't get another chance to talk with Bud. I was so late that I had to be on my best behavior for the rest of practice.

Another great thing happened that day besides Bud talking to me. Ms. Dyre asked if I would have some free time after football season. She asked if I'd like to work on the yearbook staff. She also offered to let me help make up the school newspaper's pages starting in November.

In the afternoon, the clouds piled up and got very dark. The halls of Middlebrook High turned shadowy, even with all the lights on. I kept thinking what it would be like for a 100-member riverboat to try to move in mud. Mud is one of the worst things that can happen to a marching band. When you try to turn while playing an instrument, the ground slides out from under you. By the time classes ended, everybody was worrying about it.

"Do you want to ride with me tonight? Or,

would I be interrupting something between you and the almighty Joel?" Elaine asked sarcastically. "Maybe we should walk and stay out of the traffic jam by the school," she added. "Ryan and I are going out afterward, but I thought we could see each other on the way over."

I grimaced at her remark about Joel, but I said, "Fine, if you want to walk in the rain."

"It won't rain," she said, as if her words could make it true. "My squad can't possibly handle that wheel if it rains, so, it just won't rain."

"I wish I could believe you," I told her. "I bet he wishes he could believe you, too." I nodded toward Mr. Cavatina, who stood beside the door of the band room with a worried expression on his face.

There was a fine mist falling when we walked home, but it stopped before the game started. The field was wet, but not muddy, for pre-game. There was thunder and lightning during the first quarter, but not a drop of rain fell. I began to believe Elaine had a good prediction service. Mr. Cavatina looked anxious as we piled out of the bleachers to get into the halftime entrance formation. I thought that after this morning, Bud might talk to me, but he hadn't looked my way during the entire first half. Maybe Cynthia had scared him.

"Watch my signals!" Mr. Cavatina called through the bull horn. "We'll keep marching unless it's a downpour."

We were lucky. The rain held off through the halftime show. Bill and the majorettes did a perfect job, and the riverboat formation went well. You could tell from Mr. Cavatina's expression that he was proud of us. People in the stands applauded loudly. It was great to be there.

In the third quarter, the storm finally let loose. Nobody had time to wallow in our glory, because we were too busy wallowing in the mud on the way back to the band room. Joel and I were standing by the refreshment stand when the rain started.

"Oh, no!" Joel cried. "My clarinet is on the bleachers!" He dashed for the bleachers to grab it. We were about 30 yards from the band bleachers, but by the time we got there, we could hardly see. I grabbed my sax and ran for the safety of the building.

Horatio wasn't harmed. I dried him out well, and put him away. The wooden clarinets were the ones in the most danger. And there weren't many. *Who can afford real wood ones, except for Joel and Elaine?* As soon as the rain slowed, I put on my jacket and went out to watch the rest of the game. It was so muddy! By the time the game ended and we had lost by the score of 7-3, the field was a mess. The players looked like swamp monsters from a late night horror movie. Most of the fans had gone home, but the band stuck it out, even if we couldn't play.

"I'd walk with you," Joel told me, "but if you don't mind, I'd rather go home and get into something dry."

"I want to do the same thing," I agreed.

"Is it okay if I pick you up around 7:00 for the concert tomorrow?" he asked.

"That's fine."

I went to the band room and got Horatio. There was no sign of Elaine. She must have left with Ryan. I told her I might walk with Joel, and she tossed her curls at me. So, I wasn't surprised that she didn't wait. *Oh, well,* I thought, *it's only two blocks.*

"Do you want a ride, Pockel?" Bud called. Cynthia, hanging tightly onto his arm, gave me a look of hatred, but I just smiled innocently and thanked him. The three of us got into his father's station wagon. Cynthia scooted into the backseat with Bud, while I climbed into the front, next to Mr. Brandis. I didn't mind, though. I just couldn't believe that Bud had invited me along.

"You're lifesavers," I said to Bud and his dad. "I thought I'd be walking home in this."

"We can't have that happen to a sax player," Bud said. "Besides, I might need another debate idea someday."

I grinned to myself. He was really grateful to me. Cynthia didn't say a word. It was as if she refused to admit I was there.

"I was glad the rain waited until after the show," I told Bud.

He chuckled and gestured toward the drenched window. "This would have been horrible," he agreed.

You can't do very much talking during the short, two-block ride to my house, but I did pretty well. When Mr. Brandis stopped the car, I jumped out, grabbed my sax from the backseat, and then said, "Thanks a lot, Mr. Brandis. Thank you, too, Bud. Bye, Cynthia." Then I hurried inside. It was still pouring rain, but I didn't feel one bit cold and wet anymore.

Seventeen

JOEL arrived at my house 15 minutes early. We sat in the backseat and talked during the long ride to Walden. Joel's mom and step-dad were driving us to the concert, and picking us up afterward.

I told Joel that I wanted to ask Walter about more science fiction books. Joel shook his head. "Now I have two friends who are out of this world," he teased. "What's so great about those books?"

"I like the exciting adventure," I said.

His parents dropped us at the front door, and we barely got to our seats beside Walter and his date, Carol, before the concert started. The conductor raised his baton. It became dreadfully silent. And from the first note, I was captured by the music.

Before the intermission, I noticed that Joel was holding my hand. I honestly don't know which one of us reached for the other.

I'd heard the *1812 Overture* before. But that night it seemed like the orchestra took me on a tour of the battlefield. I was there, smelling the smoke-filled air, watching the fighting.

We still had some time after the concert, so we all went to Burgers Plus in Walden for a snack. I ordered french fries and an orange soda. We talked about school, band, and music. And just as Joel had warned me, Walt loved to tease.

While we waited for Joel's parents to pick us up, I asked Joel why nobody ever teased him.

"I beat them to it," he said easily. "Mom got all the short jokes when she was in school, and she had to learn to take it the hard way. When she realized that I was going to be short, too, she prepared me for what was to come." He paused, and then he said gently, "Walt really likes you, Ginger. Otherwise, he wouldn't bother teasing you."

"I know. I'm sorry I don't take it well."

"You'll have to think like my mom. She told me she tried to see herself as being tall enough to look down on everyone. If she thought that she was tall, then others would, too, she believed."

We drove home, and Joel's parents let both of us out at my house. Joel told them that he'd walk home from my house. We stood on the curb and waved as they drove away.

It was nearly midnight when Joel took me to the door. "Do you want to come in?" I asked.

"No, it's late." He looked at me for a minute, and then without warning, he kissed me. There ought to be a better way, a more romantic way to say it than just, *he kissed me.* It was not like anything I ever expected. There were skyrockets! Cannons! Smoke! Anthems!

And then, suddenly, I wanted Joel to stop. I could see Elaine frowning at me. And I could see Bud, offering me a ride last night in spite of Cynthia. Joel was not acceptable. He spent all his time practicing music. He didn't have time for this. And I didn't want to fight with my best friend. I had to stop this before I liked Joel too much. I pushed him away.

He just stared at me. His eyes clouded, and he frowned. After a minute, he spoke in a voice that was a little harsh. He said, "I'm sorry, Ginger. I thought you.... Well, it doesn't matter, I guess." He turned around and walked down the steps.

I started to call to him, but his name got stuck in my throat. *Well, Ginger?* I asked myself. *What will you say if you do call him back? You're sure you don't want to get involved with this guy, aren't you? Then you don't have anything to say to him.*

I went inside and listened through the closed door until I heard his footsteps fade away.

Eighteen

WHILE I was waiting for the bus to come on Saturday morning, I couldn't stop thinking about Joel. Was he angry or hurt, or both? And why should I care? I didn't want to become involved with him in the first place, did I? So, why did I accept his invitations? Why did I let him kiss me? Why couldn't I sleep last night?

I got on the bus and reminded myself that this was all for the best. I couldn't keep seeing him, even if I really wanted to. I couldn't do that to Elaine.

Elaine has been my best friend since third grade. While I rode downtown I remembered the sixth-grade play, when she was a princess and I was a tree. She knew I wanted her part, and she went to extra trouble for me. She was the one who suggested we work out our parts together. I can still see us sitting in her bedroom, trying to think of ways to make a tree noticeable. In our imaginations, I got struck by lightning and fell on the handsome prince. I spread my limbs and flapped them in the breeze until it looked like a hurricane, and when all else failed, I uprooted and replanted myself right between the prince and the princess. When the day of the play arrived, I didn't do anything odd. I was a perfectly ordinary tree, and Elaine was a wonderful princess. But by then I didn't mind being a tree. When Elaine took her bow, she grabbed my limb to make me bow with her.

These days, Joel had Elaine worried because her clarinet position meant a lot to her. She also disliked Joel intensely. She thought he was arrogant and self-centered. I didn't want to think about whether I agreed with her. I reminded myself that Elaine was my friend. I didn't want to lose that friendship over Joel. Joel wasn't that important to me. As a matter of fact, he wasn't important to me at all. *Was he?*

This was no time to think about this. I clutched my purse. Inside was the classified ad that I had taken from the back of the paper I gave to Bud. I had attached it to a copy of my band article.

I walked into the *Brookview Chronicle* and

stepped up to the counter, hoping that my voice wouldn't squeak.

"Um, Mr. Marburn asked me to come," I said to the woman behind the desk.

She smiled. "Shall I say who is calling?" she asked as she lifted the telephone receiver from the desk behind her.

"My name is Ginger Pockel."

The woman spoke into the mouthpiece. "A Ms. Pockel is here to see you, sir. Shall I send her up, or have her wait?"

She put down the telephone. "It's the second floor, on the right," she smiled and pointed to the elevator. "Go right into Mr. Marburn's office."

When I stepped out on the second floor, I noticed frosted-glass windows on the doors that were closed on either side of me. I gently opened the one marked "Editor," and took my story out of my purse and unrolled it.

"Mr. Marburn?" I asked.

He looked up from his desk and gave me a brief smile. "Are you Ms. Pockel?" I nodded. "Please sit down," he gestured with a wide, chubby hand. "I'm glad you came. Are you interested in newspaper work?"

"I think so," I said. "I did a story for my journalism class."

"So you said in your letter. Is that your

story?" He reached across the desk, and I handed it to him.

Mr. Marburn settled into his wide chair, and looked through it, while I tried not to fidget.

"This is a nice feature," he said. "Thanks for bringing it." He sat forward and folded his hands on top of my story. "What intrigued me, though, was your letter. You were right. We simply cannot afford to hire after-school, part-time people."

Disappointment surged up inside me. I thought how glad I was I hadn't mentioned this to anyone. I also wondered how I was going to get out of here gracefully. I nodded.

"But you brought up a good point about wanting to know what it would be like to be in newspaper work. Did you say you go to Middlebrook High?"

"Yes," I said. I couldn't figure out why he'd called me in just to tell me that he couldn't hire me. I guess it was a really stupid idea.

"What grade are you in?" he was asking.

"I'm a freshman," I managed. If he would let me go, I'd get out of here as quickly as possible.

But Mr. Marburn said, "Your point was good. There isn't any way to know whether you'd like this work, except to do it. Your letter reminded me of an idea that I've had for a while, but have never pursued. The idea is to start a high school page, with input from each of the city's high schools. It would discuss what's going on in high school besides sports. We already cover the sports, as you probably know."

"If I could get a reporter from each school to provide a column every week, I think we could make it work. Are you interested?"

I hardly knew what to say. "Sure," I told him.

"That's good. Why don't we try it out then? Try to work up a column or two about your school. I'll see what I can get from the other schools." He took out a handkerchief and polished his glasses, and then he settled them back onto his nose. "There would be no pay for this, you understand. But you and the other writers would be first in line for summer jobs. What do you think?"

I couldn't believe what he was saying. I could barely manage to stammer my thanks, and promise to have something for him by the following Saturday.

"Good." Mr. Marburn stood to shake hands. "Now, let's hope that eager journalists in the other five area high schools will be interested. I'll start looking on Monday." He paused, and then he said, "Pockel is your last name. Are you Bill Pockel's daughter?"

I nodded.

"Then I'll expect really good things from you."

I walked out, on feet that couldn't have come close to the floor. It wasn't a job, but it was an adventure. Now I was glad that I wrote that letter about getting started in journalism.

Ever since the day I wrote that story, I'd been thinking that there must be something I could work on as hard as Joel did on music. Now I couldn't wait to tell him. But then I remembered. After last night, Joel probably wasn't even speaking to me. Well, I could tell Mom, Dad, Ms. Dyre, Elaine, and Bud about my adventure.

As I walked into McRaftrees Department Store, I noticed people walking by with closed expressions. I wanted to grab someone and say, "Hey! Look at me. I'm a journalist with my own column."

That thought stopped me for a moment. A woman bumped into me, grumbled, and went around me. *Did I really want to be a journalist? What about my parents? I was doing what they wanted me to do. Well, it wasn't a career. It was just a tiny column. I didn't have to decide my career for a long time. For now, it felt wonderful to see if this was what I wanted. I didn't need to fight my folks just because they wanted the same thing that I did.*

Elaine was waiting for me at the restaurant on McRaftree's third floor. We sat there for awhile, looking out wide windows that overlooked the river and the city park.

"How was today's lesson?" I asked her. She's taken clarinet lessons every week for as long as I can remember. After she finishes, we usually get together to do something.

She shrugged. "It was fine. Mr. Sterrett says that I can probably get into the university orchestra when I'm in college, even though they normally allow only music majors in."

"You aren't going to major in music, are you, Elaine?"

She covered a yawn. "No, I wouldn't be one of *them*. I think I'd like to be a chemist. But that's still years away, anyhow. Did you go to the concert last night?"

I smiled. "Yes, it was wonderful!"

"It was wonderful, even with His Majesty there?" she asked.

"We had a good time," I said. I could have told her how I ruined everything with Joel, but I didn't want to. I waited until our lunches

147

arrived before I spilled the news about my job. Then I couldn't talk about anything else. I told her about the building, the office, Mr. Marburn, the newspaper's new high school page, and what I planned to write about. Then I realized I was doing all the talking.

"Oh, I'm sorry," I said. "I guess I'm kind of excited."

"I thought you didn't want to do what your parents wanted you to do," Elaine said, sounding faintly bored.

I tried to tell her it wasn't my parents' idea, but she just smirked. "Sure, Ginger. You just don't see what they're doing. I'm happy for you, but don't get carried away. When you're 30 years old, do you want to only be writing about life while others are living it?"

I grinned. "What's the big deal? If I really decide to be a journalist someday, then that *will* be living. And right now, all I'm doing is a high school column. It doesn't mean anything is decided at all."

Elaine thought I was crazy to spend my time writing. But she could spend all day in the chemistry lab, and think that was fun. To change the subject, I asked, "Do you want to go look around at clothes?"

She agreed unenthusiastically. Something was bothering Elaine today, but I couldn't figure out what it was. I tried to cheer her up by telling her about the music at the concert. I talked about Walter and his passion for science fiction.

Elaine just made some crack about my hanging around with strange people.

"Walt's a concert pianist," I said. Elaine is also a good pianist. Walt couldn't challenge her, so she could appreciate him.

"Is he from Northbrook?" At least she sounded interested at that. "I may have heard of him."

Everything that afternoon seemed to make Elaine mad. She didn't like the clothes that we tried on. And when I bought a novel that Walt had suggested, she told me I was going to turn my brain to mush.

"Mushbrains from Mars," I said. "It sounds like a good title to me."

Somewhere between Juniors and the record department, I finally asked her what was wrong.

"What's wrong with *you*, Ginger?" she exploded at me. "You've turned into someone I don't even know. You're running around with Stockwood, who is going to challenge me. You're reading weird books and picking up a whole bunch of crazies for friends. And now you're just doing whatever everybody wants you to. What happened to the Ginger who used to be my best friend? And I never thought you'd start going with Joel, that little creep. You have to do everything you can to prove you don't want me for a friend!"

I gasped, but she continued. "Why Joel Stockwood, for heaven's sake? It's like you deliberately wanted to slap me in the face. You could have chosen *anybody* else."

"What's the matter, Elaine? Are you afraid he's better than you are?" I snapped. The words slipped out before I could stop them.

"I suppose that would make you happy, wouldn't it? You'd like to see me bumped down in band by that hotshot. And I thought you were my friend."

"Elaine, I didn't mean it!" I cried, but she already walked off. I went after her. "Look!" I yelled as I grabbed her arm to stop her. "What difference does it make whether he beats you or not in challenge? You both play first clarinet music. My gosh, Elaine! Do you have to be the best in everything? He's a music major. He ought to be better than you are. You're a chemist. You said so yourself!"

She set her lips and glared at me. "Let go of my arm!" she yelled.

"Elaine, my dating him shouldn't make any difference to you. I'm not challenging you.

Whatever argument you have with him shouldn't have anything to do with you and me."

I paused, and she glared at me. Then I thought of something that had been bothering me. "But while we're at it, you might remember that I am dating him. I'd appreciate if you'd cut out the insulting remarks, at least when I'm around."

Elaine stuck her nose in the air. "Don't worry about it, Ginger Pockel. If that's the way you feel, I'll make sure I don't talk to you about Joel Stockwood, or about anything else, either." She wrenched her arm from my grasp and stormed off.

I stood in the middle of the store, feeling terrible. I'd just lost my best friend. And I'd lost her over a guy who I'd spent the past two months pushing away from me with both hands. After the way I acted last night, he probably would never talk to me again, either. Now in defending him, I'd lost Elaine. *Why did I defend him anyway?*

I headed for the bus stop. Maybe I could apologize to Elaine, never speak to Joel again, and have my friend back. But that was wrong. I knew it was wrong, even if I never dated Joel again. Then at the words "never date Joel again" my throat constricted, and I felt empty inside. That's when I knew that Joel was my trouble more than anything else.

I really liked Joel. All those days talking with him after band and seeing him at lunch. Then there was the Homecoming Dance, the bike ride through the park, the concert, and his kiss. All those moments came flooding back to me.

All that time I had let Elaine make nasty remarks about Joel, and I'd done nothing to stop her. But at the same time I was looking forward to seeing him, enjoying our conversations, and laughing at his jokes. I didn't think Joel was arrogant at all, especially after I'd heard him play. Everything he said about himself was true. Elaine just didn't want to believe it.

"Boy, what a jerk you've been, Ginger," I muttered as I stepped onto the bus. "Now that you've practically told him that you don't care about him, you realize you really think he's terrific. You never should have let Elaine's mixed-up anger keep you from making up your own mind."

Now that I understood all of this, I was more upset than ever.

Nineteen

BY the time I got home, I was hurt and angry. The more I thought about Elaine, the angrier I got.

She didn't want me taking anyone else's advice, but she wanted me to take her advice about Joel Stockwood. I had believed her when she said he was arrogant. I had even agreed with her.

But after I'd heard him play the clarinet, I realized that he had a right to brag. Maybe he didn't even brag enough. Elaine was wrong, and I wasn't going to beg her to forgive me. If I'd lost my best friend, then the price was too high to keep her.

And what was wrong with my writing a column for the newspaper? I was proud of it. If it happened to her, I'd be happy about it! After all, I didn't make cuts about her wanting to be a scientist. I was grateful because she made a great lab partner.

So why couldn't she let me try to find out what I wanted to be? No, I was not going to feel guilty about Elaine.

As soon as I was in the house, I called to Mom and Dad, "Can I talk to you two?" Dad was watching a ball game on television, and Mom was in the kitchen. But there must have been something about my voice, because Dad switched off the TV and Mom came right in.

I plunged right in with my news. "I went to the *Chronicle* office today. Mr. Marburn asked me to write a column for Middlebrook. He wants to start a high school page. And the best part is that if I do well at it, he said he'd consider me for a summer job."

"Why, that's wonderful, Ginger!" Mom started, but I stopped her.

"Now, this does not, I repeat, not, mean that I'm making big decisions about what I'd like to do someday as a career. It's just exciting to find out for myself what it'd be like. Will you both promise not to push me with this?" I paused a minute, and then I added, "Please?"

Then Dad asked, very gently, "Do you feel like we push you, Ginger?" There was a hurt expression in his eyes.

I couldn't say yes, even if I did think so.

"Ginger," my mother said quietly, "we're very proud of you. We'll be proud of whatever you do. We know you like to write, but above all we just want to see you enjoy yourself. We really don't mean to push."

I didn't want to hurt them. I was ashamed of myself, because now they'd worry forever. I shouldn't have made them feel bad about being supportive. "Well, I wanted to tell you," I said. Then I went upstairs because there was too much water in my eyes.

That's a perfect score, Ginger, I told myself. In less than 24 hours, you've said or done things to hurt practically everyone who is important to you. I flung myself onto the bed and cried. It didn't matter that I kept telling myself that I shouldn't be crying.

After a while, Mom came up and said, "Ginger, will you tell me what's wrong? Besides us, I mean?"

"Oh, Mom, I've done everything wrong. This morning I was so happy when Mr. Marburn gave me the chance at the column. But then I had a fight with Elaine. And then I was unfair to you and Dad. I just can't seem to do anything right anymore."

She sat down on the bed beside me. "It's hard growing up, Ginger. It's scary to take on new things and to bring new people into your life. When two people are as close as you and Elaine are, it might be confusing. But don't you see? Having different interests or different friends doesn't mean that you still can't be the best of friends."

"But, Mom, she absolutely can't stand Joel. And all she does is put him down." I blew my nose. "She's mad because I'm dating him, and she's really scared inside that Joel's better at clarinet. She thinks I've joined the enemy camp or something."

Mom frowned. "That doesn't make much sense, Ginger. Unless you gave her the impression that you did join an enemy."

"No, she doesn't make any sense when it comes to Joel. I tried not to give her any sort of impression. But when I didn't say anything, she just kept insulting him. That wasn't fair. When I tried to tell her that, she decided I had chosen between them. And now she's not talking to me. I was so worried about not making Elaine mad that I wasn't very nice to Joel. Oh, it's all so mixed up!"

"He's special to you. Isn't he, Ginger?"

"Oh, he's nice to be around..." I started, but then I stopped.

I was through with lying. "No, Mom, you're right. He *is* special. I just realized today how much I really like him. But now it's too late.

After the way I acted last night, he'll probably never talk to me again."

She smiled at that. "Well, since he *is* special, let's hope that won't be the case. But if it is, then you've learned not to be influenced by others when you choose your friends."

She shook her head. "I hate to see this happen after you and Elaine have been friends for so many years. Does it have to come down to a choice? You can still be friends with both of them, even if they don't become good friends."

"Well, I've thought about that, but Elaine seems determined that it's got to be him or her," I said.

When I came down for supper, my father beamed at me. "The star reporter! I'm not pushing, am I?" he asked in such a cheerful way that I giggled.

"Don't worry, Dad. I'll tell you if you are."

Then he said seriously, "I want to say that I have no doubts that you can do the job. I really am proud of you."

I thought of my argument with Elaine, and I didn't feel very proud of myself at all. I wished I could feel as good as Dad did. At the moment, I had a great new job, but I'd lost two good friends.

Later that evening, I finally got up my courage and dialed Joel's number. I nearly put the receiver down before I finished dialing, but I made myself do it. His mother answered.

"This is Ginger Pockel," I said. "Is Joel there?"

"I'm sorry, Ginger. He's been working all day, and he went out for a bike ride. Should I have him call you?"

"No, it isn't important," I told her. *But it was important.* I felt empty and cold inside, and I wondered whether he went riding *alone.*

Twenty

ON Sunday, I began listing all the clubs and people I needed to contact for news items. I organized my calendar according to the Saturdays when the columns would be published. I listed organizations and their advisers or presidents. Ms. Dyre would know any names that I didn't. But I didn't want the column to become just a list of events.

"What's the matter with you, Ginger?" I asked aloud. "You're supposed to be excited about this, and already you're making it seem dull."

There was no one to answer me. Mom and Dad were busy. Then I realized I was listening for the telephone to ring.

I wondered if Joel had gone out alone last night. Or, had he found someone else already? Why didn't he return my call? I just couldn't call him again. I didn't have the courage. If

*he didn't want to talk to me, I couldn't force
him, could I?*

I told myself to be happy. I tried to
remember how I felt yesterday at the
Chronicle office. I had been scared when I
had to face the receptionist and Mr. Marburn,
but when I came out, I was sure I could tackle
anything. Well, now that I did have
problems—*big problems*—I'd have to handle
them myself. No one could do it for me.

I stood up and marched over to the telephone. At first, I started to dial Elaine's number, but I put the receiver down. Then I
picked it up and dialed again. I'd spent a
good part of last night learning that I had to
live with my own opinions, and Elaine had to
live with hers.

"Mrs. Runyan?" I began, and nearly fal-
tered.

"Oh, Ginger!" she recognized me. I could
feel the warmth of her smile right through the
line. "I forgot to tell Joel that you called. Hold
on, and I'll go get him."

After a brief pause, Joel answered. "Hi!"
he said breezily. "Mom just said you called
last night. What's up?"

I had a brief surge of panic. I didn't have
the slightest notion of what to say, or why I'd
called. I guess I just wanted to hear his voice,

to have another chance to see him. I wanted to know that he wasn't mad at me. "I, oh, nothing," I stammered, and then I took a deep breath. "Look, I was wondering..." I gulped, and then asked, "would you like to come over?"

"Gosh," he hesitated, and then added slowly, "I don't know, Ginger. I've got a lot of work to do this weekend." My heart sank. Obviously, he was through with me. "How about 3:00?" he went on. "I couldn't stay long, though. I've got so much to do here."

I could have danced around the room, but the phone wouldn't reach. "That's great!" I told him. "I just—just want to talk."

We hung up. I went down to the kitchen. "Joel's coming by at 3:00," I said. It was hard to sound casual. Mom looked up and smiled. Yesterday, I might have been insulted by that look.

I put on my apricot top and gray slacks. I wondered if it was too dressy. Joel's favorite color is blue. I changed to jeans and a blue blouse, and I looked in the mirror. I looked so pale that my face had a purplish cast. I put on a white top. I decided it was too dull. Finally, I went back to the apricot and gray. By the time I hung everything up again, it was almost 3:00. I went downstairs. Mom was making brownies, and the whole house smelled great.

"Chocolate?" Dad sniffed appreciatively as he came into the room. "Somebody must love me around here." Mom grinned and pulled the pan from the oven just as the doorbell rang.

Joel stood on the porch in his blue jacket, grinning. I wanted to grin, too. "Do you want to take a walk?" he asked, and then he stopped as I opened the door. "Do I smell brownies?"

That made me laugh. "I'll get my coat, while you go help yourself to a brownie." When I came back, he was clutching a brown lunch sack protectively.

"Your mom gave them to me, honest," he said, "and I didn't even have to beg." He turned to my mother. "We'll be back in an hour or so."

We walked down to the park. But now that Joel was here, walking beside me, I didn't know what to say.

He broke the silence. "You look nice in that color."

"Thank you," I answered, but it wasn't what I wanted to say. We hadn't touched. He hadn't taken my hand. We veered off the path that was crowded with bicyclists and late-autumn joggers, and we wandered beneath the trees past the picnic tables.

Joel cleared his throat and started tentatively, "I was surprised when you called. Um—the other night I got the idea...." His voice trailed off.

"Yeah, well," I said. *Where were all those words I could come up with on paper? It was as if I'd forgotten the English language.* I finally managed to get the words out. "Joel, I've been doing a lot of thinking this weekend. I guess I've been letting Elaine do too much of my thinking for me up till now, and...."

"What are you talking about? What does Elaine have to do with this?" he interrupted sharply.

"She hates you!" I blurted, and I felt my eyes brim beneath the contact lenses. "Well, maybe she doesn't hate you, but she's sure upset with you. I think she's jealous. She keeps making me feel like a traitor for dating you. And she's threatening not to be my friend anymore. But, Joel, I do like you!"

Oops! I hadn't meant for it all to come spilling out like that. *Now he'd despise me for sure,* I thought. But Joel got this funny, puzzled look on his face, like he was trying to figure out what I was saying. Then, suddenly, he hugged me close to him.

Then he put his hand under my chin, tilted my head back, and kissed me. It was the kind of kiss that said that everything would be okay. But it also turned on the orchestra in the bushes. I always laughed at those old movies when the hero kisses the heroine, and the orchestra starts playing. But I swear I heard it that day, and I resolved never to laugh at those movies again.

A little while later, we began walking again, holding hands. "If I had known you called me yesterday, I'd have called you back," Joel said. "I spent the weekend wondering what I did to make you not like me."

"I spent the weekend doing lots of thinking and trying to figure out what's important to me," I said, and then I told him my big news about the newspaper and about my fight with Elaine.

Joel was excited about the newspaper column. He kept congratulating me over and over. "I knew it! I just knew you were a great writer." He beamed.

But after a while he got serious again. "Ginger, I don't like being the cause of your fight with Elaine. You two have been good friends for a long time, haven't you?"

"Yes," I admitted. "But, Joel, I can't always do what she wants. That's the easy way, but it doesn't make me happy. I knew you were too important to me, and I knew you'd never ask me to make a choice like that. I still can't even figure out why you scare her so much."

Joel grinned. "I make her nervous. She's never had any real competition before. I know she doesn't like me. But maybe she will someday. Don't be so hard on her, Ginger," he said. He squeezed my hand. "You know, I doubt Elaine's ever been able to tell you what to do. Don't give up on her. I've got a feeling your friendship with Elaine will last for a long time."

He was right, I realized. "But she *is* being unreasonable," I pouted.

"Oh, that's okay. Maybe she'll change her tune when I challenge her. You know I want her position, don't you?"

"Joel Stockwood! Don't you do this to me, too!" I shouted, which caused a few joggers to turn and stare at us.

Joel winked and casually slung his arm around my shoulder. "I'm teasing, Ginger. I won't put you in the middle. Elaine shouldn't have either."

"Well, I don't want anything to do with either of you in that battle," I declared happily. "I'm staying out of clarinet matters."

"Those matters, perhaps," Joel agreed, "but don't stay away from this clarinet player anymore."

Twenty-one

IT felt odd to go to school Monday morning without waiting for Elaine. But I had yesterday afternoon with Joel to think about and to keep me company.

I missed Elaine. I missed her good humor and her cheerfulness. But I went to our locker and was glad not to meet her there. I wasn't ready to talk with her. I might love Elaine like a sister, but this was important.

Bud was in the hallway before band started. I told him a little about the column, and then asked him for a schedule of the upcoming debates. "Will you keep me posted if the team should, say, win the district finals and go on to state competition?'

"You're working for *The Chronicle?*" Bud asked. "How'd you get a position like that, Pockel?"

Elaine would have been sophisticated and

casual, but I just couldn't. Instead, I grinned like a cheshire cat, and said, "I asked for it." Then we had to hurry to reach the band room.

Mr. Cavatina handed packets of music to the alternates to pass around to the sections.

"We have a special arrangement this week. Since it is the last football game, this show will be in honor of our seniors. It's a jazz arrangement of an old song, *Memories*. The arrangement and all the parts were written by Joel Stockwood in the advanced harmony class."

I gasped and stared at the handwritten music, and then I glanced over at Joel. But he was busy handing out copies.

Mr. Cavatina rapped on his music stand and said, "Well, let's find out how it sounds."

"If it stinks, does he flunk the course?" Bob Stewart asked, and we all laughed.

Mr. Cavatina smiled blandly. "I don't think I'll say."

The music *was* good. I was impressed. The show was easier than last week's. Part of it was a salute to the seniors. The ceremony was impressive enough that some of the girls got teary the first time we ran through it outside.

Joel hadn't told me about the arrangement. Now I understood why he had so much work to do over the weekend. But why hadn't he talked about it?

When band period ended, I hurried to put Horatio away and look for Joel. The bell rang, and I knew if I waited much longer, I'd be late for my next class. Finally he came out of the band room, but as I started toward him, Cynthia stopped him.

I watched her tilt her head in that coy way she has. Her strawberry blond curls caught the light from the stairway window and seemed to sparkle. As I watched her speak to him, I couldn't deny that she's pretty. Joel smiled, and he looked at her closely. Even at a distance, I could see that. As I hurried down the hall, I realized that I was jealous. There was something in that look she had given Joel. I'd seen it somewhere before, but I couldn't remember who or.... Well, it didn't matter, anyway.

"Ginger!"

I heard him, but I was afraid to turn around. *Suppose Joel had changed his mind since yesterday, and Cynthia was hanging onto his arm?* I didn't want to see them.

"Is this space taken?" Joel asked, smiling.

"What space?" I watched my feet.

"The one beside you, of course." He was alone.

I gulped. "It's reserved for someone special, and I think you might qualify," I told him. Then, I couldn't resist asking, "What did Cynthia want?"

Joel shrugged. "She's star-struck, I guess. She didn't really say anything."

"Why didn't you tell me about the music, Joel?"

"Do you like it?"

"I think it's super! But why...?"

"I didn't know Mr. Cavatina would use it until this morning. I wasn't sure whether he'd like it. And if it turned out to be really horrible, I didn't want my best girl to know." He grinned happily. "Besides, I wanted to surprise you. I didn't know about *your* writing either until you won the award."

"That's not fair," I told him, "because I didn't know until then either. You've always known you're a musician."

"Yes, but I didn't know whether I could learn to arrange music," he said. "That was my main reason for coming to Middlebrook, remember? Of course, I didn't know then about the fringe benefit I'd find here." He grinned.

* * * * *

There was a quiz in physical science, so I didn't get to talk with Elaine at all. But I knew we couldn't share a locker all year in stony silence. A couple of times during class I looked in her direction, but she was bent over her paper doing problems. And as soon as the bell rang, she grabbed her books and took off. I started after her, but she met Ryan outside the door, and they walked away together.

I spent lunch period racing all over the building, talking with the Latin Club president, the drama coach, and the Student Council president. I also added some dates to my calendar. By the time I got to journalism class, I had a sizable list going, and some new details on the Winter Fair. After class I told Ms. Dyre about the column.

"What a good idea, Ginger. That shows real determination," she said enthusiastically.

"Ms. Dyre," I said, "I don't want this to become just a list of activities. I want it to be a real column."

She looked at me. "It's your column, Ginger. If you want it to be read, then you must find things that appeal to both the students and the adult community in general. You might consider doing one interview a week, and then ending with a list of events."

"Of course!" I agreed. "I should have thought of that myself."

I thought I'd be the last person in the building, but the band room hallway was still full of students. Then I remembered that the photography teacher was taking pictures of the senior band members for the yearbook. Some of the others had stayed to watch.

Joel had Elaine backed against our locker and was talking to her, and he had a serious expression on his face. I was about to join them, but suddenly someone grabbed my arm and spun me around.

"Pockel? Ginger, I mean." I looked up at Bud. Behind the glasses, his eyes were wide and very brown. "Hi," he said.

"Hi," I said. "Have you been watching the seniors?"

He nodded. "Listen, uh...."

I was hoping to see Elaine. If he had some news about the Debate Team, I didn't want to take notes right now.

"Um, will you go to Winter Fair with me?" he finished. Suddenly, it seemed that there was silence all around us.

The chattering voices seemed to quiet as I took a minute to understand what he had just asked me. *Here it was*, I realized, *the invitation I'd been wanting for three years*. I couldn't believe it. I thought of—of nothing. I couldn't even remember why I had wanted to date Bud. I could never think of anything to say when we met in the hallway. And then there was Cynthia. I thought of the way she looked at Bud, and in a flash, the light poured into my brain. That was what Bud saw in Cynthia. She gave him hero worship. It was the same look she gave Joel this morning. But it wasn't something I could do for Bud. I'm not made that way.

That made me think of someone else. It made me think of yesterday in the park, bike rides, walks, concerts, and laughter. I thought of someone who could cheer me up when I was in a crummy mood, and someone with whom I never ran out of conversation. I suddenly realized how dumb I'd been all year, chasing after Bud.

Those thoughts all popped into my head in about half an instant while I collected the words I wanted to say. Then I said, "Gee, Bud, you're great to ask me. As a matter of fact, I think you're a great guy. But I'm afraid I have a special guy now."

"Oh," he said, "I didn't realize—" It would have been so easy to embarrass Bud right then, and get back at him for the teasing I'd taken. But I didn't want revenge. Bud *is* a nice guy. There was no point in hurting his feelings.

"It's perfectly all right, old chap," I said in my best British accent. "Keep a stiff upper lip and all that. There are lots of other branches on your tree." I thought a moment. "Some have pretty nice limbs, too."

He just grinned. Then I walked down the hall to find out what Elaine and Joel had been deep in conversation about.

Joel was at his locker, but Elaine was waiting for me.

"Elaine, I—"

"No, let me speak, Ginger," she said. "I'm sorry. I was out of line. Joel just gave me a good talking to. I hate to admit it, but I guess he's right. I don't want to let Joel, or the clarinet section, or anything else get in the way of our friendship."

"Elaine, I don't want to lose you," I told her, trying not to blubber before I got it out. I hugged her, and for once I think even Elaine didn't care how sophisticated she looked. She was crying, too.

"I guess I thought if he was a threat to my spot, then he was also a threat to our friendship," she admitted.

"I felt terrible this weekend," I admitted. "It must be okay to have two best friends."

Elaine grinned and wiped her eyes. "He said he didn't want to come between us. You know, he *can* be very nice. Maybe I just didn't give him a chance."

"You didn't," I agreed, "but don't start tossing those curls around at him. I couldn't stand you as a rival."

"Don't worry," she said, "but you can tell him for me that I'm not giving up first-chair clarinet without the hardest fight he's ever seen. He'll have to be super to beat me out of that position."

"Tell him yourself. I'm not getting into that fight—again," I laughed, and took her handkerchief to wipe the tears from my eyes.

"What did Bud want with you?" Elaine asked curiously.

"Oh, he just wanted to take me to the Winter Fair," I said. "I turned him down."

Elaine gasped.

"Are you two feeling better?" Joel asked. "I thought I might walk home with you two tonight."

"Uh, I've got some errands to run," Elaine smiled. "You two go on."

"I'll call you later, Elaine," I said. As Joel and I started toward the door, I turned to him. "Whatever you said to her really helped, Joel. Thank you."

He shrugged. "I just told her the truth, the whole truth, and nothing but. Hey, speaking of the truth, did I see you talking rather seriously with Brandis? What'd he want?"

"He asked me to the Winter Fair," I said matter-of-factly, "but I told him I had a date with a special guy. Do I?"

Joel grinned. "I guess you do, heartbreaker. Poor guy, he may never be the same after being turned down for a short guy like me."

"You, sir, are just the right height." I took his hand. "Notice how our hands fit right together." I paused. "Actually you may be interested to know that I was very nice to Bud. You might say I handled his feelings, uh, gingerly."

Joel laughed. It was a merry, sweet sound like music to go with the twinkle in his eyes. "You, my dear, are outdoing yourself today. I think all this good news deserves something special. Let's make a special trip to Cyndy's Soda Shoppe to celebrate with a bottle of...." he waited for the frown I couldn't help. Then he finished triumphantly, "ginger ale."

About the Author

VICTORIA M. ALTHOFF lives in a family of storytellers. She especially likes hearing, reading, and telling stories about courage and humor. She often gets ideas from her husband, David, who was the hero of her first story, and from their children, David and Christopher.

Victoria loves words. "I like to play with them, say them, roll them around on my tongue, and make them my own." She learned this love from her father, who is a poet. She also enjoys people, especially young people. "Students I meet are vibrant, exciting, and interested in life. I'm enthusiastic for the future they will bring us," she says.

When she's not writing, Victoria works as a production editor of college textbooks. She has also been a newspaper reporter, a city-planning technician, and a technical writer and editor.

At home in Columbus, Ohio, Victoria enjoys music, sports, taking walks, and reading. Her favorite books include mystery, adventure, and of course, romance.